ANGEL'S halo

FOREVER ANGELS

USA Today bestselling author
TERRI ANNE
BROWNING

Angel's Halo: Forever Angels
Written by Terri Anne Browning
All Rights Reserved ©Terri Anne Browning 2018
Cover Design by Sara Eirew Photography
Cover Picture by Wander Aguiar
Model: Shane Mac & Megan Napolitan
Edited by Lisa Hollett of Silently Correcting Your Grammar
Formatting by M.L. Pahl of IndieVention Designs

ISBN : 978-1797546797

10 9 8 7 6 5 4 3 2 1

Table of Contents

PROLOGUE

TANNER

Three weeks earlier

Twirling my little brother's keys around my finger, I whistled as I walked out of the clubhouse toward his truck. Warden was already sitting in the front passenger seat, meaning I was going to hear Raider bitch all the way to his woman's house and then to Raven's.

Raider was bigger than Warden. Longer. Meaner. Warden had his moments, but mostly he was a whiny little bitch. Still, he was grabbing things for some of the other females currently camped out in the main room of the clubhouse, which meant I didn't have to. I could put up with the bitching to get out of that shit.

Opening the driver's door, I climbed in and sat, my fingers drumming on the steering wheel as I waited impatiently.

The front door of the clubhouse opened, Raider's large frame coming through the opening, and I started the engine…

It stalled before catching, and my gaze locked with one of my best friends'. We both knew what was going to happen next. My heart dropped into my stomach, and I started counting down the seconds in my head.

Fuck this shit.

I opened the door, jumping out just as the boom shook the world. The force of the blast sent me flying, white-hot flames searing my back as my front connected with two cars parked by the fence, and I fell between them. My head bounced off the asphalt, and I groaned in agony seconds before blackness consumed me…

I cracked my eyes open as I felt myself floating. The smell of gas hit my nose at the same time the godawful pain made itself known. There wasn't a single part of my body that didn't hurt, but the worst was coming from my back. I could feel the blisters, the pain coming off them so intense, I was surprised I wasn't in shock from the agony.

Maybe I am.

I was surrounded by darkness, but my eyes slowly adjusted, and I realized the floating sensation I was feeling wasn't just from all the pain. I was in the trunk of a car which was moving at a speed that made me think we were on the interstate.

Fuck, I hurt.

I twisted, trying to get my big body into a better position that didn't hurt as much. Bad idea. The worst I'd had in a while. Just breathing hurt; why the fuck did I think moving would make it any better? It was so intense, I saw stars, my stomach heaving from the agony. I managed to turn my head enough that I didn't choke on my own vomit.

Knew I shouldn't have eaten all those eggs.

The puke made me cough, which had me gasping for my next breath from the torture my body was sustaining. It was too much, and I blacked out.

A sharp slap across my face had my eyes snapping open. "Fuck off," I growled.

Two men stood over me. One of them I knew well; the other I'd only seen from a distance. I was lying on something cold, but the coolness did nothing to relieve the burning on my back. My hands were strapped down, as were my ankles, the way the ties cut into my flesh telling me they'd gotten rid of my boots and socks. My shirt and cut were gone too, but at least I still had my jeans on.

"You gonna arrest me, Sheriff?" I smarted off, pretending like I wasn't in the worst pain of my entire life. I was good at pretending. It got me into trouble. A lot. But trouble was fun. Mostly. This, not so much.

"Got better plans for you than that, Reid," Bates said with a smugness on his bulldog-like face. "Fontana paid me good money for your worthless ass. Lucky me, I found you stuffed between two cars while your pussy MC brothers were bawling their eyes out thinking you'd burned up in that truck with the other fucker."

Warden.

Fuck.

A different kind of pain tore through me, but I swallowed it down. Now wasn't the time to mourn my MC brother. I currently had other problems screaming for my attention.

The other man's face pushed closer to mine, his breath heavy on the garlic. I blinked my eyes at him, trying to focus through the haze of bad breath. "Back the fuck up, and get yourself a mint. Go ahead. I'll wait."

Fontana punched me in the stomach as he straightened, his face pale with rage. The hit knocked what little breath I had out of my lungs, making me wheeze and cough. The agony that was my back protested, and I had to blink back the darkness attempting to flood over me for the third time.

"Reid here has a mouth on him," Bates informed the Italian seething over me. "Sometimes you have to shut him up before you can get the answers you want."

The chuckle that left me felt like it was going to kill me, but I wouldn't let these bastards see how weak I really was. "I'll talk all you want," I assured him. "Whaddya wanna talk about, Bates? The way your momma was sucking my dick last night? You want to talk about that? She's got a mouth on her, man. The way she gets on her knees and blows me…so damn good."

Creswell Springs's sheriff had ham hocks for fists, and they both connected with my jaw, one after the other. I laughed, fighting the urge to throw up as the action only made me want to scream in misery, and then spit the blood that was filling my mouth at him. "Your momma hits harder than you, fucking little bitch."

Another punch to my jaw and I felt one of my molars break off. I spat it out, and it landed on the floor at the sheriff's feet with a tiny *ping*.

Damn, I just got that tooth fixed too.

The last time it broke off was in the same fight where my little brother broke his arm. Damn college kids thinking they could come into Hannigans' and play pool with the big boys. We showed them quick why the Reid brothers were unbeatable. They'd gotten a few good punches in and fucked up Matt's arm before I took a pool stick to their heads.

Fontana was back in my face, his breath burning my nose hairs. "I like that you're a talker." His voice was chilling, but it took a hell of a lot more than him to make me shiver. "It shouldn't be too hard to get the information I want out of you."

This guy was hilarious.

I might have been a fuckup at times. Running my mouth and causing trouble was what I was known for. But this prick was never going to get a single secret out of me about my MC brothers.

"Really wish you'd get that mint, man," I grumbled. "And maybe lay off the garlic sauce. You're adding to the ozone problem. Don't you care about global warming?"

A muscle started to tick in Fontana's jaw, and I found the energy to smirk up at him.

The smirk turned into a grimace—the only thing I was willing to give him to show any sign of discomfort—when he punched me in the side.

Something told me my liver was the least of my worries with this guy.

CHAPTER ONE

Present day

I could see my breath in the cold night air, but I was numb to the chill attempting to distract me.

Beside me, dressed in black from head to toe just like me, including the paint on his face and the hood over his blond hair, Jet gave me a nod.

I glanced at the night sky again. It was cloudy, keeping the moon at bay and offering us cover from the enemies within the multimillion-dollar mansion in Eureka, just two hours from home. Static filled the earpiece linking me to my MC brothers, Ciro Donati, and Cristiano Vitucci.

Both men had wanted to be there when we took down Fontana. They showed up with ten of their own men, ready to help us destroy the motherfucker who had caused us all so much pain and grief in the last few months, but even more over the last three weeks.

Three weeks since Tanner and Warder met the Angel of Death from the bomb Fontana hired one of our prospects to hide in Matt's truck. Then the bastard shot up the bar and cost us Uncle Chaz, sending Uncle Jack into a massive heart attack that killed him almost instantly.

And Fontana shot Lexa.

My rage was already burning bright, but remembering how my baby girl caught a stray bullet because of that motherfucker had me craving blood.

"Move in on my command," Vitucci's voice growled in my ear. "Three, two... Let's go, boys!"

I kicked open the side door to the mansion. The place was unimpressively secure for a man who should have been counting down to his last heartbeat. He should have known that I would come for him, that I would kill him with my bare hands if I got to him first.

Instead, he'd been shacked up in this mansion on the California coast, with only three other men to watch his back. No one patrolling the grounds. One lousy camera overlooking the garage, and windows wired with alarms. It hadn't made sense when Colt first reported what he found when he, Jet, and Spider followed Hank Badcock here the week before to find out if Badcock's lead was correct. But after stalking the house for days now, no one could figure out why the place was so insecure.

Like they wanted us to blow in.

Like they wanted us to show up on their doorstep looking for retribution.

Or they were cocky as fuck.

Lucky for us, Colt's woman'd had people in higher—or maybe even lower—places than we did. Badcock had come to check on her and brought us the little gem of information about Fontana's possible location.

There was no one in sight when Jet and I entered the house from the side door. No sound meeting our ears except for the heavy breathing of the others or the kicking in of more doors. The artillery in our hands went unused as we cleared room after room, looking for signs of Fontana and his men.

A gunshot filled the air from above on the second floor. Hawk cursed in my ear then laughed wickedly. "This one's gone," he muttered.

Two more shots, then all was quiet again.

Only three?

Where the fuck was Fontana? The others would have said something if they'd found him first. They knew he was mine. That I wanted to do to him what Adrian Volkov had done to his brother.

"Fuck." I heard Donati growling. "Made it to the basement. Get your fucking asses down here."

"Oh fuck," someone groaned before the distinct sound of puking filled my ear. "That smell," he gagged. "Is he dead?"

Cautiously, Jet and I made our way downstairs. Harsh gasps in my ear followed by curses loud enough to be heard without the aid of the device greeted me with each step we descended. When we got to the last step, we found at least fifteen men in the basement, some of whom were standing in puddles of their own vomit.

All of these men had seen some heavy shit in their lives without flinching. What was so bad that they lost their stomachs over it now?

The scent of their bile hit me, but I ignored it, pushing past my MC brothers, two of my brothers-in-law, and some of the men Vitucci brought with him.

I stopped before I reached Donati. I hated the bastard—even now jealousy churned in me as I remembered watching him on his date with Raven all those years ago. But in this kind of situation, I trusted him.

The look on the man's face in that moment, however, gave me pause when our gazes locked. Blue eyes the same shade as Flick's darkened in a way that confused me. Since when did this emotionless monster have compassion in his soul?

Then his gaze moved, sliding to the table behind him, and almost helplessly, my eyes followed. The first thing I saw was an IV dripping from a coat hanger. My eyes traced the line to an arm that lay at an awkward angle. It was obviously broken, and in more than one place by the looks of it, but the bruises were so bad on the man laid out on the table, I couldn't even tell what ethnicity he was.

A new scent that wasn't vomit hit me when I took a step closer, and I suddenly understood why there were so many puddles of puke on the floor.

Rotting flesh was one of the worst smells on the planet, and right then, it was coming off the man on the table in waves.

The poor fuck.

Flies buzzed around the body as I examined it closer. His other arm wasn't mangled like the first, but he was missing his pinkie finger, the skin charred from where they'd burned the wound closed. It lay beside him, as if his torturer wanted to taunt him with it, along with all of his fingernails that had been pulled out at the roots. The guy was shirtless, and my eyes caught on the ink of his chest.

I felt the bile begin to rise in the back of my throat, but I swallowed it down.

No way.

It wasn't possible.

He died.

The explosion took him from us just as it had Warden.

Yet...

I knew that ink. Had been with him when he let Spider brand it into his skin. The angel wings with the cross in the middle in memory of his parents.

Blinking to clear my vision, I looked at the man's face. A beard I'd rarely seen on my cousin mixed with blood and fuck knew what else. His face was pale, his lips cracked, blood dried on an open gash. Part of his left ear was missing, as if someone had been hacking away at it and got bored. One eye was swollen closed, pus oozing out of it.

None of that explained the scent of rotting flesh, though.

Donati lifted the body, shifting it to show me and the others the blistered and blackened skin of his back where maggots feasted on the decayed flesh.

The bile threatened again until I felt someone behind me. Donati carefully replaced the body back on the table at the same time I heard a pained wail coming from my cousin's lips as Matt pushed past me.

"Tanner!" He screamed his brother's name, shaking his arm. "Tanner? How are you here? Oh fuck, what did they do to you?"

I should have pulled him back, made him go upstairs, and not allowed him to look at his brother's dead body like this. But I was unable to make my legs work. All I could picture was that flaming truck, where Tanner and Warden had burned to death after the blast of the bomb nearly leveled the compound. People saw him in there. Raider saw him before the blast knocked him on his ass.

So how the fuck was he here, in Fontana's safe house basement?

A weak cough filled my ears, and everyone in the room stopped breathing.

He was alive?

How was that even possible?

"Ah, fuck." Tanner's voice was barely above a whisper, sounding pained, maybe even drugged. It was hard to tell what was in the IV that was feeding fluids into his arm. Fuck, they must have been keeping him alive to get information out of him. His dry lips moved and the gash cracked, blood beading on his lips. "Matt, man. Did they get you too? Are you dead?" A tear spilled down Tanner's cheek. "Did we end up in hell together, little brother?"

CHAPTER TWO

 TANNER

I was pretty sure I was hallucinating.

Again.

Why else would I be seeing my baby brother standing over me crying?

Matt didn't cry. Not even when I hit a baseball straight into the back of his head when he was five and he needed seven staples to close the wound. Not even when Mom and Dad died. Neither of us did. The tears were there, but they never fell.

It wasn't the first time I'd imagined people I loved beside me. Matt. Bash. Raven.

Her.

Fuck, I wished it were her.

I was glad to see my little bro, even if I was sure he wasn't real. But I wanted her image back. Her smile filling my eyes as the Angel of Death finally took me away from this shitshow.

The pain was still there. Not as intense thanks to all those kick-ass drugs Fontana and his little bitches kept pushing into the IV they'd used to draw out my death, hoping I would finally break and give them something. Anything other than my smartass mouth telling them to suck my dick or to at least bring their mommas in to do it for them. The morphine or whatever they kept feeding me only took the edge off, though.

The agony of my back was what told me I was still among the living. The smells coming from me told me it wouldn't be long. I smelled the death already invading my body. The decaying flesh of my back, the flies that buzzed around, annoying the hell out of me, laying their eggs in the rot.

But it was her face that kept me going.

And it was her face that I wanted to see when I finally let go.

Jos.

Fuck, I miss her.

Too late to remember it was my fault she hadn't been by my side the past two years. I pushed her away after letting her get too damn close. I was such a fuckup, and her dad didn't want her to be a part of the MC life. She deserved more than what I could give her.

Goddamn, I wish I could kiss her one last time.

"Tanner." Matt was speaking again, and I had to focus on the words leaving his mouth. "Hold on, brother. Hold on. We're going to get you to the hospital. You're going to be okay."

I barely noticed how his voice cracked, how his hands shook as he and Bash—Bash was here too? Hell yeah! We were going to have a party before I kicked the bucket—lifted me carefully.

The breath hissed out of me as the flesh on my back protested, and I blinked in surprise. The pain was just as miserable as always, yet my brother and cousin didn't disappear or glitch before me.

Wait.

"Are you really here?" I asked Matt, my voice so weak I barely heard myself.

"Stop talking," Bash commanded, but his voice cracked just like my little brother's. "Save all your energy. I swear, you're going to be okay. I don't care what we have to do to save you."

"I'm too far gone—" I tried to protest, wishing they would just let me rot.

"Shut up, Tanner!" Bash wasn't my cousin now, but my MC president barking orders. "You're going to be fine."

Sighing, I closed my eyes, craving the sight of Jos again. When the image of her under me filled my mind, I focused on her and only half paid attention to what was going on around me.

"Get the door," Matt's voice boomed. "Get the fuck out of the way."

Jos's soft hands touched my cheek just as I was laid out on something cushiony. Matt's voice kept telling me to hold on as he lifted my head and put it in his lap. I heard tires squealing before the vehicle they'd just put me in jerked forward. That floating feeling filled me as Jos told me she loved me—but that wasn't a memory.

Just another hallucination.

She'd never said those words, but her eyes had always confessed her feelings for me.

I felt my heart begin to beat a little slower than it already was. Jos's face began to glitch behind my lids, and I felt a tear spill from my eyes.

"I love you too," I gasped, unsure if I said the words aloud. "I miss you."

"Drive faster!" Matt roared. "He's fading."

Really wish he would stop screaming in my ear.

My breaths became shallower, and it was taking everything I had just to draw another one. I knew the end was close. I'd felt the Angel of Death breathing down my neck for a while. He was clouding my vision now, his dark, hooded figure blocking out everything.

Jos's face began to fade completely.

No!

Her beautiful face flashed across my closed lids again.

"Don't leave me," I begged her, feeling my tears come fast. "Stay with me. Don't go."

"I won't," Matt answered, and I wanted to yell at him I wasn't talking to him, but I couldn't make my mouth work. My throat was closing. "I'm right here, brother. I'm not leaving you."

Jos.

I wanted her so fucking bad. Loved her so much, my soul had been holding on by its fingernails in the hope that I would see her for real one more time.

"Tanner!" Matt was screaming in my ear. "We're almost there. Please, please, just hold on a few more minutes, and then we'll be there. Bash, fucking drive faster."

"I'm already doing a hundred and ten! I don't know where the fuck I'm going."

"Then do a hundred and twenty! He's dying."

"Jos," I whispered. "I'm sorry."

CHAPTER THREE

 JOSIE

I jerked awake when a hand touched my shoulder. Gasping, I sat up straight on the little mat Reid and I had been sharing the last few nights in the main room of the MC's clubhouse.

Reid grumbled in his sleep, turning on his stomach, sticking his little butt in the air, and letting out the kind of sigh only the sweetly innocent were capable of.

My eyes focused on the man crouched beside me, and my heart began to calm slightly. "Daddy?" I whispered, so as not to disturb any of the others sleeping on their own mats close by.

With the MC on full lockdown, all the families were now calling the clubhouse home.

There wasn't much room left for anyone else, even in the main room.

Dad's eyes were wide awake when they met mine, a guarded look on his face that told me something was wrong. Lifting his finger to his lips, he waved his hand, indicating I should follow him.

Tucking the thin blanket up over Reid, I carefully got to my feet and followed. We walked through the kitchen, which even now was alive with some of the women making coffee and whispering. They all shut up the second I entered the room, and as soon as the door closed behind us, I was pretty sure the conversation picked up right where it left off.

What the hell is their problem?

I got that I'd messed up. Royally, spectacularly. The kind of fuckup that couldn't ever be undone because I left telling Tanner about his son too long. I was going to have to live with that for the rest of my life. It broke my heart to know my son would be without his father through all the huge milestones in his life, just as much as it broke my heart that the man I'd once foreseen spending eternity with was dead.

Stop it, Jos.

I quickly shut down my mind on those thoughts. They could choke me with guilt later. For now, I had to see what my dad wanted that was so important he woke me up before dawn.

Outside, Raven was pacing back and forth, her phone to her ear as she listened intently. On either side of the path she was wearing out the asphalt on with her boots stood three of her four future sisters-in-law. Seeing me with Dad, Flick shared a quick look with Quinn and Gracie. It was Quinn, sweet, pregnant Quinn, who stepped forward and pulled me into a hug.

I blinked, unsure what I was supposed to do with this. Growing up with a mother who thought hugs made a child spoiled and without my father around, I didn't experience a lot of physical contact outside of the snuggles Reid loved so much.

On Raven's next turn, she saw that I had joined the group, and she abruptly ended her call with a sharp, "We'll be on our way soon."

Quinn stepped back as Raven pushed the phone into Flick's hands and approached me. Her face was set in hard lines, but when she reached me, I saw that she was fighting back tears. I might not have known her well, but one thing I did know was that Raven didn't cry for no reason.

Seeing those tears set my nerves on edge. "What's wrong?"

She swallowed roughly and grabbed my wrists in both hands, squeezing so hard it was painful. "The guy who killed your grandpa and blew up Matt's truck?" I gulped, a flash of white-hot pain searing through me, but I nodded. "Bash took some of the brothers to deal with him. They got everyone but the guy responsible. Chickenshit must have known they were coming."

"Was anyone hurt?" I whispered thickly.

She shook her head, but two tears fell down her cheeks. "No. But…" Her inhale was shuddery, and I felt the tremor all the way to her fingertips, the aftershocks rocking up my arms. "But they found one of our own in the basement."

I nodded, unsure what she expected me to say about any of this. If the man responsible for Grandpa's and Tanner's deaths wasn't already on his way to hell, then what did any of this have to do with me?

"It's Tanner," Flick suddenly announced, stepping up closer to me.

Anger rocked through me, and I jerked my wrists out of Raven's hold. "I know what I did was wrong, and I'm well aware everyone in this MC thinks I'm a total bitch, but you two don't have to be cruel."

Quinn and Gracie came up behind me, blocking me in, and I suddenly felt claustrophobic. The four of them were ganging up on me. My dad was still pissed at me, and something told me he wouldn't help me out if these women suddenly started beating the shit out of me.

Quinn's soft hands touched my arm. The kindness in her eyes made a lump fill my throat as the same tears in Raven's eyes spilled out of her blue ones. "She's not trying to be cruel, Jos. I swear. None of us believed it either when Jet called earlier. Flick yelled at him and told him not to come home if he was going to play sick jokes like that. But then Hawk sent Gracie a picture of Tanner in a hospital bed. It is...bad."

"But you told me he died!" I exploded, breaking through the wall they had built up around me.

There was a weight pressing down on my chest, making it hard to breathe, and I knew I was seconds away from having a full-on panic attack. I hadn't experienced one in years, not since that first time with Tanner. He'd grounded me, made me fall for him even more as he'd held me through the mind-bending panic after my mom called to scream at me over something trivial.

And then he'd made love to me.

Or, as he later described it, fucked me good and nice.

That was after I'd asked him if I could stay in Creswell Springs with him forever. After I'd seduced him for the second time in the two weeks since he'd first taken my virginity. I'd done some things I wasn't proud of to get his attention back on me after our first time. Flirted with some not-so-nice guys, pretended like once he'd popped my cherry, I didn't mind who fucked me as long as I got dick.

It was all a lie, though, a ploy to make him jealous—to see if I even could—and to make him mine again. It worked, but after that last time, he treated me like trash, and I walked away with a broken heart. Finding out I was pregnant with Reid had scared the living hell out of me, but I wasn't about to put any of us through the same crap I'd grown up experiencing firsthand. I wouldn't use our son to hold on to Tanner. I wouldn't control Reid by giving him ultimatums about when he could see his father or make him feel guilty if he ever picked his dad over me.

I took on the role as single parent, even though I was sure Tanner would have stepped up and helped me raise our child.

Looking back on it with hindsight, I saw how scared I'd been of being rejected by the man I'd stupidly fallen in love with. Again. I didn't want to go through that over and over again when we exchanged diaper bags and car seats at the end of every other weekend and holidays. I had been selfish, and now we were all paying for it. But it was Reid who would suffer the most, and it broke my heart.

"We thought he did!" Raven yelled, then visibly forced herself to calm down. "We all thought he had, Jos. Raider saw him in the truck before it exploded. The coroner said there was no way of knowing who was who when it came to Warden and Tanner because there was nothing left but ash. We never questioned it. I don't know what happened, or how, but he's been in Fontana's goddamn basement for three fucking weeks, and he's close to death now. The doctors aren't giving him good odds."

The panic was only increasing with each word out of her mouth. I bent in half, my hands on my knees as I tried to suck in a breath. He was dead. Then he was alive. Now he might actually die.

I couldn't bear it if he died a second time.

Raven's cold hands touched my back, rubbing soothingly. The surprise of the action gave me the tiny bit of control I needed to draw in my next shallow breath. "He's asking for you," she murmured, so softly it was almost tender. "He keeps saying your name…among other things, but Bash said it's obvious he's wanting you."

"M-M-Me?" I whispered, dumbfounded. "Why would he ask for me? He hates me."

"I don't know. But every time he speaks, it's your name. We need to go. It's a two-hour drive."

"But…" I tried to think past the possibility that Tanner actually wanted me with him right then. "Reid is asleep. I need to get him ready and—"

"I'll take care of Reid," Quinn assured me. "He likes me. We've played a lot with Max the last few days. I promise, I'll take care of your son as if he were my own. And your dad will be here. We won't let anything happen to him, Jos. I swear to you."

I sucked in a deep breath, but it did nothing to calm me. Leave Reid? No. No. No. I couldn't. We hadn't spent a night apart, ever. He needed me. I needed him. He was all I had.

"Tanner needs you more than Reid does right now, Jos," Raven told me, her eyes darkening with impatience. "We have to go. The longer we wait, the higher the chances we get there too late for him to even see you."

Tears spilled down my face instantly. "Okay," I cried. "Let's go. Quinn, please take care of him." I needed to go now before I changed my mind and ran back in for Reid.

"I will. Don't worry. You just focus on Tanner."

Raven and Flick pushed me toward the black SUV across the parking lot. No one said a word as the two women climbed in the front, leaving me alone in the back for the long drive to whatever hospital my baby's daddy was currently fighting for his life in.

CHAPTER FOUR

I was shaking by the time we got to the hospital. Raven pulled up in front of the ER, and there was an MC brother there to park her car for her as we walked inside.

People I didn't recognize surrounded those I did, all of them dressed the same, with black army-like paint smeared across their faces like they'd all just come from a weekend of playing war or some shit.

Jet stepped forward with Hawk, both of them embracing Raven and Flick before turning to me. "He's in real bad shape, Jos honey," Jet informed me, his face tense yet grave. "They have him in the ER right now, trying to clean out the flesh…" He broke off when Flick made a distressed sound, and he hugged her against his side, pressing her face into his cut. "But he keeps asking for you. Maybe if you are with him, you can make this a little easier on him."

I squeezed my hands together, trying to get some small trace of warmth back into them, and nodded. "I'll do whatever you need me to," I assured him. "Just show me where to go."

Hawk took my arm, guiding me past the ER desk where the nurses gave us kind nods, past full exam rooms and curtained-off areas where the less serious patients were being taken care of. I heard someone groan, as if they were in absolute agony, and I whimpered.

"Tanner?" I whispered, and Hawk nodded grimly.

"It's not pretty," he warned. "You are about to see and smell something that will haunt you, sweetheart. But try to keep it together for his sake, okay?"

"Okay," I said with a gulp.

"Good girl," he murmured and knocked on a door at the end of the corridor.

Seconds later, it opened, Bash standing there with tears in his magnetic eyes so like his cousins'. He was so tense and angry-looking, I instinctively took a step back. Noticing my reaction, he attempted to ease his expression into something less intimidating, but he didn't really accomplish it.

"Thank fuck," he breathed and grasped my free arm, forcefully pulling me into the room.

The instant I stepped through the door, it was like being hit by a wave of the worst-smelling scent on the planet. I gagged, trying to breathe through my mouth, then my nose again. Neither helped, and I had to cover my nose and mouth with my hand.

"What is that?"

"It's rotting flesh," a voice I didn't recognize answered. I glanced over and saw a man in scrubs with a mask on and a light blue gown tied around him. He looked like he was performing surgery, and I couldn't be sure he wasn't.

"Tanner has second-degree burns on his back," Bash explained. "It's mostly healed, but the rotting flesh has been infected with maggots. The doctor said that was probably the best thing to have happened to him since they've fought off gangrene setting in. But he's cutting away the rest of the rotten skin."

He had scissors in one hand, tweezers in the other, as a nurse helped him clean Tanner's back. Tanner lay facedown on the bed, two different IVs in his arms pushing fluids and medication into him. Oxygen was in his nose, the heart monitor connected to him letting us all know that his heart rate was very, very low.

The doctor cut away something on Tanner's back and placed it in the container another nurse stood holding patiently.

"Are you Jos?" the doctor asked casually as he continued to work.

"Y-Yes."

"Then please, come sit beside the bed," he requested. "Our friend here is on the strongest meds we can possibly give him, but they can only do so much. He keeps talking about you. Maybe he's talking *to* you. Not quite sure right now. But I think he needs you more than he needs me at the moment."

Matt moved from where he'd been standing in the corner of the room, startling me so much, I jumped. When I didn't move quickly enough for him, he picked me up several inches off the ground and carried me over to the chair the doctor indicated. Sitting me down, Matt stood over me, waiting to make sure I didn't run away.

I really, really wanted to run away.

Tanner groaned again, his body flinching with pain, and I instinctively reached out. My hand touched the side of his face, my fingers stroking over the weeks' worth of beard on his jaw, my thumb touching his deeply cracked lips.

"Shh, shh," I murmured softly, as if I were talking to Reid having a bad dream. "It's okay. I'm here."

His eyes opened to mere slits. They were glazed with narcotics and pain, and he blinked a few times, as if trying to focus on me. Then he smiled a sad, heartbreaking smile, and my world stood still. "I really must be dead this time." His words were slurred but not unintelligible. "Never believed in heaven before, but I'm glad I got here."

Tears poured from my eyes, but I rushed to reassure him. "No, Tanner," I choked out. "You're not dead. I'm here."

He lifted his hand slowly, as if he wanted to touch me. I had to swallow my gasp when I saw he was missing a finger, and the tears only fell harder. I caught his hand, brought it to my face, letting him feel that I was real.

"Even when you cry, you're beautiful," he mumbled before his eyes closed again, and he let out a harsh groan.

"Why the fuck aren't you doing this in an operating room with him knocked out?" Hawk demanded from where he was still standing by the door.

"Because he wouldn't survive going under," the doctor told him calmly, but now I could see the sweat soaking through his scrubs and the surgical gown. It was beaded thickly on his brow. His voice and hands were steady, but this was getting to him just as much as the rest of us. "Your friend here has a mean burn on his back that's scarred up pretty thickly, and it makes it hard to numb him. Any idea where that came from?"

"My guess?" Matt's voice was little more than a feral growl behind me. "The bomb we thought killed him must have scorched his back."

The doctor made a noncommittal sound, continuing his task. Every time Tanner groaned, my heart rate jumped and I tightened my fingers around his, fighting back the whimpers of distress for him.

"Try talking to him some more," the doctor urged. "It might distract him from what I'm doing."

I turned my head, wiping my nose on my shirt before leaning in closer to Tanner. "This probably isn't the best time to yell at you, but you never seemed to hear me unless I was shouting." I stroked his beard with my free hand, scratching through the tangled tufts. "How the hell did you get in this mess? Huh?"

His eyes cracked open again, a pained smile lifting his lips slightly, making blood bead on them anew. I wiped it away with my thumb. "I'm always gettin' into trouble, baby. Whaddya talkin' 'bout?"

Matt placed a cool, damp cloth in my hand, and I used it to wipe across Tanner's lips. "You're going to have to calm that down now, mister," I scolded gently. "Your son needs you around too much for you to keep up the troublemaking like this."

His eyes drifted shut. "Whatever you say, Jos. Just sit there and touch me, 'kay?"

"When you're better, I'll bring him to see you," I told him as I kept stroking his face with the damp cloth, wiping away dirt and blood. "He looks just like you. I may have stirred up some trouble when I got to the clubhouse the other day. Rory doesn't like me all that much because of it."

"Rory?" he said with a pained grunt. "Where's Matt?"

"Right here, brother." Tanner's eyes opened enough so he could see the man standing behind me.

"Where's Rory?" he asked, sounding weak.

"Back at the clubhouse. She's okay. Don't worry about her."

"She not treating Jos okay?"

Matt sighed. "They're not fighting. Just avoiding each other. Your kid kind of took us all by surprise, man."

"There's that word again," he mumbled. "This is the most fucked-up dream I've ever had."

CHAPTER FIVE

It took another hour before the doctor was finally finished cutting away all the decayed flesh on Tanner's back. No sooner were the nurses cleaning up, than the ICU team was there to take him upstairs.

All three nurses appeared to be in their late thirties, early forties. They each had their hair neatly pulled back from their faces. Two of the three didn't even blink when they saw Tanner's state, letting me know they must have seen some crazy medical shit over the years. The third one took one look at Tanner and blanched, but she also seemed to be the one in charge.

Feeling his bed moving, he clutched at me with his four-fingered hand. "Don't leave me," he whispered. "Every time I open my eyes somewhere new, you're gone."

I leaned over him, kissing his cheek. "I'm not going anywhere," I promised.

The nurse in charge made a disapproving sound and started to say something, but the ER doctor pulled her aside, whispering something to her. Her eyes scanned over me disdainfully, taking in my pajama pants and long-sleeved sleep shirt. Both had holes and stains on them thanks to my son, but at least I had on a bra.

With a twist of her lips, the nurse gave him a nod and didn't protest when I walked with them out of the room and down the hall to the elevators.

"Jos!" Tanner shouted weakly, only to groan in pain.

I bent in the cramped space of the crowded elevator so we were on an even eye level, my hand skimming over his shaggy, dirty hair. "I'm right here. Shh, shh. I'm right beside you."

He blew out an exhausted breath. "You're so pretty."

I lifted my lips in a halfhearted smile. "Only pretty? You called me beautiful earlier."

"Beautiful. Pretty. Gorgeous. The sexiest female I've ever seen in my entire life." He seemed to lean into my hand, wanting more of my touch. I didn't know what to make of what he was saying. Tanner Reid wasn't one to go around tossing out compliments on a woman's beauty unless it was about how nice her tits were.

Seconds later, the elevator stopped, and the three nurses pushed the bed forward. I followed behind them, while Tanner kept calling my name. I rushed to keep up, following them straight into the ICU ward and to the room directly across from the nurses station. The three women worked quickly, getting him hooked up to everything again, checking both IV sites, confirming all his information through me since he wasn't in the right frame of mind to answer for himself.

Once he was finally sorted, two of the three left, and Tanner was starting to struggle on his bed.

"Jos," he growled. "Where the fuck did you go?"

I leaned over him, kissing his brow. "I'm here. Stop moving around so much. You need to save your energy."

He blew out a relieved exhale, his four-fingered hand tucking mine against his heart. "Stop fussin'. Ain't no need, baby. Gonna die soon."

I couldn't hold back my whimper. "Don't say that," I whispered fiercely. "You're not going to die. Do you hear me? I won't let you."

His smile told me how tired he was, how much pain he was really in. "Always liked it when you got all bossy. Even when you were just a little girl, you threw out orders like you owned the world."

"My grandpa was your boss. Of course, I got to order you around," I reminded him. "I guess I'm your boss for real now." At least that was what Grandpa always said. When he passed, I would take over the construction company he'd spent his entire life building up. Dad didn't want to run it, had never shown any interest in the business side of Barker Construction.

Tanner's brow puckered in confusion, but he didn't comment.

"Ma'am, I let you stay so we could get him comfortable, but there are rules here in the ICU ward. I need you to go now until visiting hours."

I glanced up at the nurse. "Why? I'm not causing any trouble. He's more comfortable when I'm close to him. Isn't that more important?"

She pressed her lips together, that disdainful look returning tenfold, and I felt insulted just from the way her eyes kept going to the spaghetti sauce stain on my left boob. I refused to fold my arms over my chest to hide it. "He needs to rest. That is what is most important right now. This is a quiet floor, with limited outside contact to help the patients recharge. You will only hinder not just Mr. Reid's recovery, but also that of my other patients."

I wanted to punch her in the face for the snide way she was talking to me, but I didn't want them to kick me out of the hospital—or worse, arrest me.

Kissing Tanner's brow again, I straightened, but he didn't release my hand. "Where you goin'?"

he demanded, his voice slurred. "You said you'd stay with me."

"I'm not going far. Just out into the waiting room. You need to sleep," I tried to explain. "I'll be back as soon as visiting hours start."

His fingers clutched at me, the stitches on the nail beds catching my attention. Would his fingernails ever grow back? I kissed the back of his hand, fighting tears.

"Don't go," he pleaded raggedly. "It's dark when you're not with me."

Twin tears fell over my lashes and onto the gown the nurses in the ER had dressed him in earlier, once his back had been bandaged. "I'm sorry, Tanner."

I tried to pry my hand free of his grasp, but he had surprising strength even in his weakened condition. "Don't go. Don't leave me here."

"I'm not," I soothed when his heart monitor started going crazy. "Baby, I'm not. I swear. I'll be right outside."

"No. Fuck that." His eyes were wild, and I ached to give in. "I want you here. Beside me."

The nurse grasped my elbow, pulling me backward roughly, and suddenly I was in the middle of a game of tug-of-war with me as the rope. I twisted my arm, pushing the nurse off me. "Don't you ever fucking touch me again, bitch." I grabbed her scrubs top and pulled her in close now that I was free, getting in her face. "I might look sweet and malleable, but you put your hands on me a second time, and you will become a patient in this ward."

The woman paled, but she didn't lose that "I'm better than you" expression on her face. "If you don't leave now, I'll call security, and you won't be allowed back."

"Jos!" Tanner roared when I started to tug my hand free again. His heart monitor was screaming now.

My mind made up, I leaned over him, stroking his brow as I tried to soothe him. "I'm right here. Shh, shh. I'm here."

Muttering under her breath, the nurse left the room in a hurry, no doubt to call security on me. They could try to kick me out, but I wasn't going anywhere. Not when his heart did scary things when he thought I was leaving him.

Fuck them and their rules. All I cared about was taking care of Tanner.

Slowly, his heart rate lowered, and I sat on the edge of his bed, stroking his face, murmuring softly to him.

His eyes were just starting to drift shut again when the nurse returned with two men in security uniforms. I eyed them both. Lean, lazy-looking. The scariest thing about them was probably the Tasers attached to their belts.

Even as small as I was, I was fairly sure I could take them both if I needed to. I worked two jobs to take care of Reid. One of them was as a bartender at a club a few blocks from my apartment in Oakland.

I dealt with guys six evenings a week, and they tended to get handsy a lot. Especially when they were drinking. Sometimes, I had to show them who was boss when they thought they could order more than just beer or shots from me.

"Ma'am, we're going to have to ask you to leave," the one on my left said. He was the nicer-looking of the two, with short, dark hair and brown eyes.

Beside him, his partner, a blond with a snarl on his face much like the nurse's, shifted as if he thought he was going to have to take me down.

I smiled sweetly up at the dark-haired security officer. "I would like to speak to your administrator in regard to filing a complaint against the nurse beside you."

His eyes narrowed, as if he thought I was only trying to start trouble, and my smile turned sweeter.

Oh, honey. You haven't seen trouble yet.

"Ma'am—"

"She put her hands on me and tried to physically pull me out of this room. Now, I don't work in the medical field, but I'm pretty sure no one is allowed to touch me unless I'm causing trouble. As you can see, she's considerably larger than me." I let my eyes skim over the nurse, who had a good thirty pounds on me. I wouldn't ever judge another person by their weight, and she wasn't fat by anyone's definition, but she'd pissed me off. "I don't think I'm much of a threat to her."

"Ma'am," the blond officer bit out. "I'm going to give you to the count of five before I pull my Taser. You're causing a disturbance on the ICU floor. I don't want to have to drag you out of here by force, but I will if you don't start listening."

"Yeah, no, that isn't happening. I want to speak to Tanner's doctor and the administrator before I even think about stepping outside this room." I stood up, but the movement woke Tanner, and he grabbed my hand, his heart monitor making awful noises again.

"Jos," he whispered brokenly.

I took his hand, but I kept my eyes on the three people in front of me. "I'm sure there is a waiting room full of big, scary men right now. All I have to do is scream, and they will all beat down those metal doors out there. Give me a reason to scream," I told the blond, leaning my head closer. "I dare you."

He looked skeptical, but the dark-haired officer moved forward as if to intercept his partner's next step in my direction. I met his gaze and nodded. "Smart man."

Shifting closer to Tanner's bed so I could hold his hand easier, I turned my gaze back to the nurse. "Doctor. Administrator. You have ten minutes to get me what I want."

CHAPTER SIX

TANNER

Jos's hand was in mine, but her body was turned away from me. Two men and a woman I didn't recognize stood before her, and from the tension coming off all four of them, I knew they were trying to take her away from me.

The skinny blond guy shifted toward her threateningly, and every instinct inside of me screamed to protect what was mine. Every movement felt like it would be the one that finally ended me, but I sat straight up in bed and pulled Jos down across my legs, using the top half of my body to protect her, cradling her back with my busted-up arm that was in a splint.

The woman shouted in surprise and rushed forward, but I lifted my head enough to glare at her, stopping her in her tracks. "Get…the…fuck…back!" I panted out, already seeing spots.

Fuck.

I was going to pass out on top of Jos. I couldn't leave her alone and unprotected from these assholes.

"Where's Matt?" I gritted out to the beautiful woman on my lap.

"He's in the waiting room," she assured me. "Tanner, please, lie back down. It's okay. No one will hurt me."

"That one would have," I nodded toward the blond security guard who was staring at me in open-mouthed terror. "Yeah, you little pussy-ass bastard. Get out of here. Go find my little brother."

"T-Tanner, your b-back." The nurse was falling all over her words, but the way she said my name confused me. Like she knew me and was upset. My gaze raked over her again, but nothing about her rang any bells. "L-Let m-me—"

"Jos will take care of me," I snarled at her, and her face paled. "Get out of here."

The blond guard was backing out of the room, his face turning green. If I looked as bad as I felt, whatever he was seeing must have been turning his stomach.

"Ma'am." The other guard was trying to stay calm. "I think it's best you get who the young lady was asking for. I'll wait for the doctor and the administrator with the patient and his friend."

"O-Okay," the woman continued to stutter as she backed out of the room, tears filling her eyes as her gaze stayed glued to me.

As soon as she was gone, Jos grumbled something under her breath. I looked away from the only remaining person in the room long enough to look down at her. "What?"

"I'm not even going to ask if you fucked her. She's so your type." Her lips pressed into a firm line, her eyes narrowed on me, and I found the strength to grin.

"You jealous, baby?"

Her jaw clenched, and she lowered her lashes so I couldn't read what she was thinking. "Maybe," she said so quietly I had to strain to hear her.

"Don't be." The spots around my vision were getting worse, and I knew I was only seconds away from blacking out. "Jos," I muttered, fighting the darkness. "Don't…leave…me."

***

The next time I lifted my eyelids, the room was dim. My heart started pounding as I glanced around for Jos.

Seeing her slumped down in a chair, snoring softly, I let out a relieved breath. Her hair was in her face, her arms crossed over her chest like she was cold. I shifted in bed, wanting to cover her with the blanket that was on me, but even that small movement made my body protest.

My involuntary groan was loud enough to wake her, and she sat up straight, pushing her hair back from her beautiful face. "What do you need?"

she whispered as she stood and leaned over me. "Is the pain worse? Should I get the nurse?"

I caught her hand in my right one and pulled it to my chest. "I'm good," I lied, pretending I wasn't in complete misery, and forced a smile to lips. "Want to lie down beside me and sleep?"

"No way," she said with a shake of her blond head. "That is your bed. You need your space and sleep. Your heart rate is starting to get better."

I scanned my eyes over the parts of her body I could see with her leaning over me like she was. The top she was wearing wasn't the one I remembered, but at least it was long-sleeved like the other one. Even in the dim lighting, I could see a stain of some kind across her amazing tits.

"You turn into a messy eater?" I teased, lifting my splinted arm so I could skim my fingers over one tit, my thumb playing with her nipple as I traced part of the stain with my index finger.

She gasped and covered my hand, pushing it away. "Funny. Don't start something you're in no shape to finish."

Sighing, I pulled my hand away, only to grasp the back of her hair and tug her down closer.

Her mouth fell open as I stopped her an inch from mine. "Just thinking about you makes me ready to prove you wrong, sweetheart."

Her lips pressed to mine, surprising me. But before I could kiss her back, she was pulling away and stepping back. "You've been in this ICU ward for five days, dummy. During that time, you've had some crazy-as-hell hallucinations and a fever that only broke yesterday. You died twice and had to be brought back. The doctors thought you wouldn't even make it through the fucking night after that first code." Tears spilled from her eyes, surprising me even more than the kiss. "When you get out of this fucking hospital, I'll let you prove it as many times as you want. But until then, save all your energy and focus on getting back to the Tanner I remember."

Her tears were killing me. "Baby, don't cry," I pleaded. "It hurts me."

She quickly wiped her eyes and nose on the sleeve of her shirt. "Sorry. I've just been really worried about you. The last five days have been hell. And every time I tried to so much as leave this room, your hallucinations only got worse."

I patted the edge of the bed, beckoning her to sit beside me. When she did, I tugged her head down to my chest, forcing her to stretch out beside me to be comfortable. "I'm sorry. But thank you for not leaving me."

"As if I could," she grumbled with her face pressed into the hospital gown covering my chest.

"What does that mean?" I whispered, my heart stopping as I waited for her answer.

The swooshing sound of a sliding door opening had me tightening my hold on Jos as a tall woman in scrubs walked into the room with determined steps. The light over my head was switched on, bathing the room in bright light. I blinked at the harshness of the fluorescent bulbs and shot the woman a glare.

"Go the hell away," I snapped at her.

"Mr. Reid, I've told you a dozen times already that the bed is for you and you alone." The woman, I couldn't tell if she was a nurse or a doctor, sounded like a patient schoolteacher trying to explain the rules of the classroom. Her face was kind and only slightly wrinkled by time. Her hair, lightly sprinkled with gray, was pulled into an old-school twist at the back of her head. She reminded me a little of Aggie, and I found myself relaxing a bit.

"Ma'am, if you had an angel who was as pretty as Jos, wouldn't you want her to share your bed too?" I asked in my best charming tone, winking up at her. Pleased when she blushed, I grinned. "Besides, it makes me feel better when she's this close."

Jos pushed away from me and sat up before standing. "Dr. Gregory, I'm sorry. I know—"

The doctor lifted a hand, shaking her head, the pink beginning to fade from her cheeks. "It's okay, Joslyn. I'm just glad he seems to be feeling better today." She lifted a chart I hadn't realized she was holding and glanced over the words before her. "I'm really impressed with the improvement he's made. His heart seems stronger now, so I would like to get ortho in to do the first surgery on his arm."

"Excuse me," I groused from the bed. "I'll just lie here and let you two talk about me like I'm invisible."

The two females shared a look, then the doctor walked over to the bed. Pulling her stethoscope from around her neck, the doctor pressed it to my chest. "I'm thinking of writing a paper on the strength and tenacity of the average MC member and how stubborn they are not to stay dead."

"I'm not the average member," I boasted with a wink.

She shook her head. "I don't suppose you are, Mr. Reid."

"Name's Tanner, sweetheart."

Jos grumbled something under her breath.

"Speak up, baby."

"I said, I'm standing right here, dickhead. Stop trying to pick up your damn doctor." She crossed her arms over her chest, glaring down at me, hurt radiating off her in waves. I tried not to grin again, but I couldn't stop my facial muscles from lifting into one.

It only seemed to piss her off more.

"You know what, I think you're doing much better." Jos turned for the door. "I'll see you later."

"Jos!" I bellowed her name, my heart pounding at the thought of her leaving. She turned to face me, a mutinous look on her beautiful face. "I'm sorry. I'll stop flirting. It didn't mean anything, I swear. Just don't go, okay?"

Her hands clenched into fists at her sides. "No. I need something to eat and a cup of coffee. I'll be back in an hour."

I sat up, ready to throw my legs over the side of the bed and follow her. The world began to spin before I could put weight on my legs, and I dropped back down. The doctor urged me back against the mattress, and I went, feeling as weak as a newborn kitten.

Dr. Gregory patted me on the shoulder. "Take it easy, Mr. Reid. She needs a few minutes to herself every now and then to eat and take care of herself. Joslyn has rarely left your side the last few days."

"Yeah," I muttered, closing my eyes as I tried to picture Jos in my head.

Fuck, I need her beside me.

It was easier to breathe when she was with me. At least when she was, I didn't have to worry about fucking Fontana. Over and over, that bastard had tried to break me, and the only time he got close enough to doing it was when he threatened Jos.

It was my own fault. I must have said her name during one of the times I was passed out, which had been often. It was a curse I'd had since I was a kid, talking in my sleep, and now it could possibly put the only woman I'd ever loved at risk.

Once Fontana had the one name that would really tear me apart, it took everything I had not to spill secrets. But those threats he made, telling me in detail how he would rape her, how he would make her scream his name and then plead for me as he ripped her in half, made me shake.

"Get her back in here," I gritted out, sweat beading on my brow. "I need her back."

The look on my face must have told the doctor some of what I was thinking, and she patted my arm again before stepping back. "Don't worry about the girl. There is an army of your brothers out in the waiting room. The two that are in here during visiting hours, especially, will watch out for her." She smiled kindly down at me. "They look a lot like you, so I'm assuming they are brothers or cousins."

"Bash and Matt," I muttered. "One of each, actually."

"They will take care of your girl. Rest until she comes back, and then you can apologize again."

Over the next few minutes, she examined me from top to bottom, spending the most time checking over my back. It did feel slightly better, but that didn't mean much.

"You're healing well, Mr. Reid," Dr. Gregory assured me. "And as I was telling Joslyn earlier, I think we should get the ortho department in to start on your first surgery. Your arm might not ever be the same again, but they will do their best to get you as close as possible."

"Will I be able to ride my motorcycle again?" That was the only thing I wanted to know. They could do as many surgeries as they wanted, as long as it meant they could fix me enough so I could ride again.

"Eventually, I'm sure," she said with a small smile. "But it's going to be a long recovery. Don't try to rush anything."

"Yeah. Okay. Now, go get Jos." I needed her back in here so I could protect her.

Sighing at my one-track mind, Dr. Gregory snapped the chart closed and pocketed her pen. "I'll see what I can do."

CHAPTER SEVEN

I finished my call to Quinn and leaned my head back against the wall outside the ICU ward's double doors.

It had been five days since I'd last seen my son, but Quinn assured me he wasn't missing me very much. Only at bedtime did he cry for me. I missed Reid so much, but Tanner had seemed to need me more than our son, so I'd stayed.

Seeing as how the first thing the asshole did as soon as he was coherent enough was to hit on his doctor made me second-guess my decision to stay with him for so long. Obviously, now that he was on the road to recovery, he didn't need me around any longer.

I shouldn't have been surprised, not with our past, but it still stung.

Ugh. I was such a stupid loser where Tanner Reid was concerned. I should have learned my lesson by now, but clearly, I was addicted to the pain he could inflict on me.

Gritting my teeth, I lifted the cup of coffee Matt had picked up at Starbucks for me and gulped down the rich brew loaded with sugary decadence.

"Can someone take me back to Creswell Springs?" I asked the two men standing across from me, not looking at either of them. They didn't need to see the humiliation that was barely hidden below the surface. The tears I didn't want to cry, the feeling of being used. Again. Of being nothing more than a body to fill the void for Tanner Fucking Reid. Again.

"Did you two argue?" Bash asked, his voice tired but calm.

"I need a shower and a few days' sleep with my son cuddled up in my arms," I told him, ignoring the question, along with that trademark Reid magnetic-blue gaze. "I'm pretty sure my hair smells like trash right now. And from the way

Quinn was talking, Reid is starting to forget what I look like."

"Will Tanner be okay while you go back to the clubhouse for a little while?" Matt asked, concerned only for his brother.

Not that I could blame him. Tanner had been my number one concern the last few days too. I'd nearly lost my mind this week while we waited to see if he was going to make it through the worst of it. The first time he coded, I couldn't keep myself from screaming in panic. The sound had brought Matt and Bash running, with everyone else in the waiting room right behind them.

Now Tanner was wide awake, thinking with his dick once again, and I wasn't needed any longer. Nothing more than a second thought. There for his needs, but forgotten the second a pretty, older face filled his vision.

"He's a grown man, Matt," I told the younger Reid now, avoiding his gaze just as methodically as I was his cousin's. "He doesn't need me around to hold his hand anymore."

"Jos, what the hell is going on?" Bash demanded now, no longer sounding calm, but frustrated as hell.

"If no one wants to give me a ride, I guess I'll call my dad." Pulling out my phone, I started to dial his number, but Matt jerked the cell out of my hand.

"Jet can take you back," he assured me. "But only if you come back later."

I lifted a shoulder carelessly. "Yeah, sure. Whatever." He didn't say how much later, and I was going to pretend that "later" meant "never."

"Go tell Tanner you're leaving, and I'll talk to Jet," Bash commanded.

As Bash walked back toward the waiting room down the corridor, I just stood there, staring sightlessly at the metal double doors. They were locked, but all I had to do was lift the little phone beside the door and ask the nurse at the desk to let me in. Some guy named Cristiano Vitucci set it up with the administrator so I could come and go as I pleased, no matter the time of day.

"I'll come back with you," Matt offered, and I jerked in surprise, forgetting he was still there.

"Do whatever you want," I told him, knowing I was acting like a total bitch but unable to turn it off.

It was all flooding back. All the reasons why Tanner and I couldn't be together. Mostly because I wasn't his type. I was twenty years old, which meant I was at least twenty years too young for Tanner. He liked them older, had always compared women to well-aged wine. The older, the better was how he saw it. Age meant more experience.

I had neither the years he preferred nor the experience he enjoyed. Tanner was my first—my only, seeing as Reid and work took up all my time and kept me from finding someone else to earn experience with.

It didn't matter that I was the one who loved Tanner. Love wasn't what he'd ever wanted, though. That much he'd made abundantly clear the last time we'd had sex before I ran back to Oakland to lick my wounds.

"Jos?" Matt touched my arm. "I'll sit with Tanner while you're gone."

"Yeah, sure," I muttered, draining the last of my coffee and tossing the empty cup into the trash can by the door. Picking up the phone, I hit "0" and waited. "I'm ready to come back in now," I told the nurse when she picked up.

"Of course, Miss Barker."

The door buzzed, and I replaced the receiver while Matt opened the door. I walked down to Tanner's room just as the doctor was coming out. Her eyes softened when they landed on me. "Ah, just who I was coming to see." She clasped my left hand, giving it a squeeze. "I wouldn't make too much of his flirting, love."

I gave her a tight smile. "Who is making anything out of it? That's just who Tanner is. So, surgery tomorrow?"

"That's the plan. There should be no issues from the X-rays, but the ortho surgeon won't know for sure until he's actually putting the arm back together." Her gaze went to Matt before coming back to me. "He seems to be in his right mind now. But just to be safe, I'll have the next of kin sign off on the surgery."

I nodded. "That is Matt, so there won't be any issues."

"Of course, you'll be here in the morning for it as well?" She didn't sound overly sure of my answer, and I didn't confirm or deny my future presence. Dr. Gregory opened her mouth to say fuck knew what, but I smiled at her and shook her hand.

"Thanks for everything, Doc. You have been such a big help the last few days."

"Jos, it really didn't—"

"Excuse us," I told her, stepping around her. "I need to tell Tanner I'm leaving. I have to check in on our son."

She said something else to Matt I didn't want to hear, so I tuned them out as I pressed the button on the wall outside the room to open the sliding door. The curtain was drawn, offering him some privacy, so I pushed it back and found Tanner sitting up in bed.

His eyes snapped open at the sound of the curtain shifting, and the frown that had been scrunching up his brow smoothed out. "Hey, don't run off like that anymore. I'm sorry about earlier. I didn't mean anything by it, Jos. I flirt to make things easier, that's all it was. You don't have to be jealous."

I shrugged. "I know you well enough to understand what you were doing, Tanner." I picked up the few things I had accumulated around the room. It wasn't much, but I didn't want to forget anything. I pulled my hair into a ponytail with the hair tie I'd left on the nightstand just as Matt walked into the room.

"Your brother is going to sit with you while I go back to the clubhouse and grab a shower and a little bit of sleep," I told Tanner and watched as the color drained from his face. I took no pleasure in the distress that filled his eyes, but I didn't have the energy to soothe him either. I was drained physically and mentally, but especially emotionally. Fighting back the sting of tears, I stepped away from the bed.

"You can't leave," he said, his four-fingered hand reaching out to me. "There are showers here. Beds you can take a nap in. Matt, find her a room so she can do what she needs to do."

"She wants to go back to the clubhouse," Matt told him. "Stop freaking out. She will be fine. Jet is going to drive her."

"No, damn it. She can't leave." His magnetic blue eyes were wild, and he pushed the covers off himself, throwing his legs over the side of the bed.

Matt pushed him back. "Take it easy, brother. Jos is a big girl. She'll be okay. Don't worry about her."

"I said no. There's no reason she needs to leave. How am I going to protect her if she's not here?"

"No reason to leave?" I repeated. "How about our son, dickhead?"

He jerked like his brother had just electrocuted him. "What the hell are you talking about?"

Matt's gaze locked with mine, and we both lifted our brows. We'd talked about Reid plenty of times for this not to be news to Tanner now.

I stepped closer to the bed, my eyes going back to Tanner. "We have a son, Tanner. His name is Reid. Is none of this ringing any bells? I've told you about him repeatedly over the past five days."

"We have a son?" He jerked against Matt's hold on his shoulders. "Where the fuck is he? Bring him here! I have to protect him too. Get him here, Matt. We can't let Fontana get to him."

"Reid is safe, man. Butch and Colt are back at the clubhouse with the other half of the brothers. Ain't nothing going to happen to him. Fontana doesn't even know about him."

"Go get my son!" Tanner roared, fighting against his brother's hold. "Go fucking get him now."

"Okay, okay." Matt tried to calm him down. "I'll go get him myself. Just relax. I won't let anything happen to him, Tanner."

He started to relax, but when I began backing away, he started to struggle again. "No. You're not leaving. Do you fucking hear me, Jos? You're staying right here where I can see with my own eyes you're safe."

"You're acting completely crazy right now," I snapped at him. "This is a hospital. Hospitals mean sick people. This is no place for a toddler to be. Do you want him to catch something?"

"I want him with me. With us. He either comes here, or I go to him. I don't give a fuck right now. I just want you and the boy where I can protect you."

I wanted to scream at him, but I clenched my hands into fists instead. "Look at yourself, Tanner. You're in no shape to be protecting anyone right now. Just let me go back to the clubhouse and take care of Reid there, where he will be comfortable and away from all the sickness of a freaking hospital."

"Matt," Tanner gritted out, his eyes hard as they drilled into me. "Call Doc. Tell him I want to be closer to home. Make them transfer me to Creswell Springs."

"Dude, you can't be moved right now. You're scheduled for surgery in the morning."

He glared up at his brother. "They have surgeons in Creswell Springs. Whatever they want to do here, they can do there. Make it happen, or I'm walking out of this place right now."

"Yeah, okay," I said with a snort.

"Jos, go talk to Bash. Get him to call Raven and make this happen." Matt was still trying to get his brother to lie back down. "We were going to have him moved closer to home once he was out of ICU anyway."

"But he's not out of ICU," I snapped at the younger Reid. "This is ridiculous. I'm going back to Creswell Springs."

"Jos…" My name was choked out, but it had more of an effect on me than if Tanner had shouted it. "Fontana knows you are important to me."

I closed my eyes, wishing it were true. It was just another one of his hallucinations, though, or a ploy to keep me where he wanted me. Tears filled my eyes, so I kept my back to him. "Then he knows more than I do," I said, my fists pressed to my chest, begging my heart to stop hurting. "I'm going back to my son."

CHAPTER EIGHT

I made it as far as the lobby downstairs before someone grabbed me from behind. I squealed before Jet's voice reached my ears.

"Easy there, girl," he grunted, covering my mouth with one of his hands. "No use in causing a scene. You want to go home or not?"

I bit into his palm, making him curse and drop his hand. Glaring up at him, I walked around him toward the entrance of the hospital. "That isn't my home." But it was now. Grandpa was dead, so someone had to run the business.

"Whatever, Miss Bitchy Pants. You want a ride, or you plan on walking?"

Seeing as his driving me was a hell of a lot faster, not to mention cheaper—meaning free—I followed him out to the SUV his sister left the last time she came for a visit and to check on everyone. I jumped into the front passenger seat and reclined the seat back enough so I could take a nap during the two-hour drive back to Creswell Springs.

But even as tired as my entire body and mind were, sleep eluded me the entire ride back.

Tanner had seemed really upset I was leaving. I didn't know if he was just hallucinating again or if he really did care that something might happen to me. But I honestly didn't know if I wanted to find out which it was.

Because I really, really wanted him to care, and if he didn't, I knew it would shatter what was left of my stupid damn heart.

Finally back at the clubhouse, I rushed inside in search of my son.

Hearing his precious giggles coming from the main room, I followed the sound and stopped when my eyes landed on him. He was toddling around, chasing after Lexa, while Max crawled right behind him. The two Reid babies could have been brothers, they looked so similar. Dark hair, blue eyes, that damn cocky set to their chin and brows. It was maddening at times, but I adored that cockiness.

As I watched, I realized Quinn hadn't just been trying to soothe my helicopter-mother feathers. Reid did seem to be having a good time without me. I put that down to all the women treating my son like their own. That was one of the things I'd always loved about my father's MC. Everyone treated each other like they were all family. All the kids belonged to everyone. They were loved and looked after, no matter where the biological parents happened to be at any given time.

"Momma!" Reid screamed happily when he finally saw me and raced across the distance separating us.

I crouched down on my haunches and waited for him to throw himself into my arms. Wrapping my arms around him, I started kissing him everywhere as I stood, making him giggle happily.

"Oh, my little man. I missed you so, so, so much." I rubbed my nose against his before kissing his cheek, inhaling the clean scent of his skin and hair. I probably smelled like week-old trash left out in the sun to rot compared to him.

"Momma," he cooed, his chubby little arms clinging to me.

Tears burned my eyes, and I clutched him closer so he wouldn't see that I was so close to an emotional breakdown. To him, I was the provider of applesauce and sippy cups. I'd never let him see me cry, and I would keep it that way for as long as I possibly could.

"Okay, wow." Raven's voice was right behind me, and I turned to face her. She put her hand to her nose. "Yeah, you were right to come back for a shower. Girl, you smell ripe."

"Ah, you say the sweetest things." I kissed Reid's cheek one more time then pushed him into her arms. "Do you mind watching him while I get cleaned up?"

"No problem. You can use my room if you want. Throw those clothes into the bedroom, and I'll put them in the washer while you shower." She arranged Reid on her hip, fingering his curls. "By the way, an ambulance is transporting Tanner from

Eureka to the hospital here right now. The guys will all be back by tonight."

"That's good news," I muttered.

"Tanner is in a piss-poor mood too, from what Bash told me."

I grunted, opening the door to her bedroom, not surprised when she followed. Shutting the door, she placed Reid on his feet and moved toward the bed to make it up. "Look, I don't know what happened, but I know that Tanner is hard to handle even on a good day. It's annoying and endearing all at the same time, and it can drive a saint to commit murder."

"Glad you know that," I told her as I walked into the bathroom and started stripping, tossing my dirty clothes into the bedroom as I pulled off each item.

"Jos, he seems to really care about you."

Naked now, I grabbed a towel and wrapped it around my body before turning on the shower to let it warm up. Standing in the doorway between the two rooms, I watched my son crawl around on the carpet, playing with a few of Max's toys he'd left scattered on the floor. "We all know Tanner doesn't go for someone like me. Hell, I practically had to beg him to fuck me the first time. And the second time, that was only because he was jealous and pissed at me. I did a lot of flirting with some of the other brothers, and I played it up enough that I got a bit of a bad reputation. But I didn't care about being called a cocktease as long as it got me what I wanted. Now I see it was all a mistake. We never should have hooked up. I was only deceiving myself thinking he would want more than a quick roll before he got bored with me. And he more than proved me right when it was over."

"Then why was he so adamant about you staying beside him when he could barely lift his head?" she tossed out.

"Because he fucked up and gave my name to Fontana?" I shrugged, remember the fear in Tanner's voice when he'd confessed. "I don't know. Maybe he has some weird hero complex, and he wants to save me from the big, bad monsters. It doesn't matter. Tanner can't love me, and I'm not going to wear out my heart on him anymore."

"But it's not like you two won't have anything to do with each other now. You have a child together. You can't keep him from his son any longer."

I would have to have been deaf not to hear the scold in her tone. Guilt slammed into me, and I nodded. "Yeah, I'm not going to keep them from each other now. And since Grandpa is gone, I'll have to take over running Barker Construction, so it's not like we are going anywhere."

She fell back on her bed, relaxing for the moment. "I'm so sad Uncle Chaz is gone, but I'm glad you're here, Jos," she admitted. Turning her head, Raven locked her green eyes on mine. "You and Reid belong with us. You know that, right?"

A lump filled my throat, making it impossible to speak. Nodding, I turned away from the door and tossed the towel onto the sink before climbing into the shower. I'd always known I belonged here. If I'd had a choice, I would have lived with Dad and Grandpa instead of Mom. But I hadn't been given that option.

The custody judge wouldn't even think about giving the two one-percenters custody of me when they tried to take me away from Mom. They had records, weren't fit to be full-time guardians in the court's eyes. But the court didn't know my mother. A pack of wild wolves would have been better parental supervision for me than that heinous cunt.

The tension in my body, along with the stickiness, was washed away by the jets, and the hot water felt like heaven. I needed to wash my hair twice before I could add conditioner, then made quick work of the rest of my body.

I didn't linger in the shower. With everyone in the clubhouse showering periodically throughout the day, the hot water never lasted long, so I knew better than to take more than a few minutes of enjoyment from the hot spray. When I walked back into the bedroom, my dirty clothes were no longer in a pile on the floor, and Raven and Reid were gone.

A fresh set of my clothes, including underwear and a bra, were folded on the end of the bed, and I dressed quickly and finger-combed my hair since Raven didn't have anything I could find that wouldn't cause more harm than good to my curly hair. Not caring about my blond curls turning into a mop, I let them air-dry as I went in search of my son.

I found him in the kitchen, sitting in a high chair beside his cousin, eating a messy plate of spaghetti. My heart melted at the sight of him covered in marinara sauce, a noddle sticking to his cheek. I snapped a picture of the cuteness with my phone, then one of Max who was just as much of an adorable mess as Reid.

As I was taking their pictures, Reid offered a handful of pasta to his younger cousin. Max leaned forward in his chair, eating out of Reid's hand. I snapped a picture of it and quickly sent a copy to Raven's phone before she could ask. I hoped these two would always be like this, that they could be best friends as well as cousins.

"Eat," Aggie commanded, pushing a plate loaded with spaghetti and crusty garlic bread into my hands. "Park your butt over there beside that baby and eat before I take this spoon to your behind, girl."

Feeling loved by her motherly gruffness, I did as she ordered. Around me, there were at least a dozen other women making plates for the rest of the clubhouse. Some of them smiled at me, but they didn't interrupt my dinner with questions about Tanner. Raven must have been keeping everyone up to date. I was glad, because I was pretty sure I would have done bodily harm to anyone who disturbed me while I inhaled the life-giving perfection of Aggie's food.

Using the last bite of my bread to wipe my plate clean, I stuffed it into my mouth then licked my fingers.

"Raven, do you think Doc will let Tanner have some spaghetti once he's settled at the hospital?" Aggie asked.

"I don't think he's being allowed solid food right now, Ag," Raven informed her. "Right, Jos?"

I shook my head. "We couldn't even get him to take broth yesterday."

"Well, I'll just make his favorites when he decides he's hungry," the old woman announced with determination.

"Good idea," Flick agreed. "We'll all help, won't we, ladies?"

They all agreed, everyone seeming eager to help in any way they could.

My phone buzzing had everyone turning to look at me. Wiping my mouth with a napkin, I pulled it out of my pocket. Seeing it was Matt, I blew out a sigh and lifted it to my ear. "Yes, your highness?"

"We will be arriving at the hospital in about forty-five minutes. Jet and Colt will bring you. Don't give them any lip."

I used my napkin to wipe Reid as clean as I could get him, noticing the red sauce had already started to stain his face and hands. "I'm sure you can oversee getting him comfortable tonight."

"Bring the boy," he commanded, ignoring my comment.

"I'm not bringing him to the damn hospital. Any mother in this room will agree with me that the hospital is no place for a baby." I looked at Raven, who was already nodding in agreement.

"Tanner wants both you and his son with him." Matt's voice held little room for argument.

Not that I would argue about it. That was just a waste of breath. I just point-blank wasn't going to comply.

"Tanner can suck it up. I'll think about coming to the hospital later, but I'm a little busy at the moment. Reid needs a bath and—"

"There are ten different women there who could give the kid a bath, Joslyn." Matt's voice rumbled.

My shoulders stiffened as I lifted my son from his high chair. "And oddly enough, I'm the only one who gave birth to him. Take good care of your brother, Matthew." I hung up and carried Reid out of the kitchen.

"You can use my bathroom again," Raven offered as she carried Max behind me. "These two seem to get along so well, and they love splashing in the bathtub together."

While Raven ran the bath, I got both boys undressed down to their diapers, tickling their tummies as I spoke softly to them both. "You two are going to be just like your daddies, aren't you?" I cooed, kissing each one of them. "You're going to break both your mommies' hearts."

Reid thought it was funny, and I attacked his belly, blowing raspberries on it. "See? Already killing me, little man."

Laughing at the boys' mingled giggles, Raven picked up her son, carrying him into the bathroom. I lifted Reid, following them. Pulling off his diaper, I placed my son in the water beside Max, offering him one of the rubber bath toys floating around.

"I can handle this if you want to head over to the hospital, Jos," Raven offered.

Using a soft washcloth, I washed Reid's face and body. "Thanks, but I've missed doing this the last few nights. We have a routine, and I'd like to do that before I go over to the hospital and deal with Tanner's bad mood."

"So, you are going, then?"

I shrugged. "As much as he pisses me off and breaks my heart, I can't stay away when he acts like he needs me." It hurt my pride to admit it, but it seemed where Tanner Reid was concerned, that pride didn't really exist. I could pretend all I wanted, but fuck, I was just glad he was alive. I would give him whatever the hell he wanted in the end.

CHAPTER NINE

TANNER

I shifted blindly in the dark room, then jerked completely awake when I felt a soft, chilled hand. Heart pounding, I found the button on the bed rail that would turn on the overhead light. Blinking against the dim, yet harsh to my sensitive eyes light, I looked for the source of the hand.

Seeing the mop of blond curls on my blanket, I reached out, shifting Jos's hair back from her face. She had dark circles under her eyes, but she wasn't as pale as she'd been when I last saw her in the Eureka hospital.

A soft snore left her, and her mouth opened ever so slightly, letting out a sigh in her sleep. I brushed my thumb down her cheek, over her chin, then her full bottom lip. A tiny smile lifted at her lips, and she pressed a kiss to my thumb.

Fuck, she was beautiful.

The way I felt about her was like an obsession, one I'd tried to deny for many years. She'd been way too fucking young the first time I'd started feeling this for her. I was ten years older than her, a grown-ass man craving a girl.

I fought it—hard.

The thought of touching Jos back then made me break out in a cold sweat. Sixteen was too goddamn young for me to even contemplate looking at, let alone touching. So I stayed far, far away. I only fucked older women, scared what I was feeling for her was a sickness that would take root and become something more dangerous.

But when she turned eighteen and surprised her dad with a visit, I couldn't fight what I felt for her any longer. I gave in, promising myself it was just going to be one time.

That first time with her had rocked me to my core, and I knew I was only fooling myself. I wanted that girl for a hell of a lot longer than one night. Forever wouldn't have been long enough.

But she deserved more than I could give her. Jos was sweet and innocent. I wouldn't be the one responsible for killing that in her.

It nearly destroyed me, but I made her leave after that first morning.

She was stubborn, though, and spent the next week flirting and going out with any brother who would give her the time of day. In a blind rage, I'd dragged her back to my house and fucked her until she couldn't remember anyone but me...

Two years ago

Matt took his shot before lifting his beer. After swallowing half of it in a few gulps, he slammed down the brown glass bottle on the end of the pool table, causing the preppy college boy on the other side of the table to flinch.

Grinning over at me, my little brother lined up his next shot, sinking the ball easily before moving on to the next one.

"This is how it's done, bitch."

Bored out of my mind, I leaned back against the wall, watching Matt have all the fun. Without my taking a single shot, Matt finished the game and then grinned wickedly, counting the money he'd just won.

Show-off.

I yawned, debating calling it a night. This place was mostly dead anyway, and I had to be up early to help Uncle Chaz pour a foundation for some guy's new detached garage. Not everyone on his crew was an MC brother. I worked whenever I wasn't on a run, and lately, I'd been staying close to home. With Matt's head still not on straight after Rory leaving him, I was needed around to keep my little bro out of trouble.

Out of the corner of my eye, I saw a flash of blond curls and froze. Seconds later, I heard a giggle that went straight to my cock. Holding my breath, praying it wasn't her, I turned slowly.

Motherfucker.

At the bar, Jos stood dressed in next to nothing. The jean shorts she wore left her ass cheeks hanging out, putting that perfect derriere on display for the entire bar to see as she bent forward, whispering into some douchebag's ear. The shirt she wore couldn't even be called that. It was shredded and knotted at her ribs, showing off the black bra she wore underneath.

All week she'd been showing up at the bar dressed like that, flirting and teasing any guy who looked twice at her.

Trying to grab my attention. Force my hand. Driving me so fucking crazy, I was about to implode from the pressure in my balls. Or explode with rage. Either would have caused a mess I wasn't sure could ever be fully cleaned up.

Somehow, I'd kept my distance, not allowing myself to take even a step in her direction because I fucking knew if I so much as smelled her perfume, I would drag her away and fuck her until neither one of us could walk. But goddamn, it had been hard. I wanted her even more than before I'd taken her home the previous week. One night with her hadn't cured me of this hunger that seemed to gnaw at my insides night and day.

The guy she was talking to put his hand at her waist, touching the skin I'd spent hours tasting and worshiping. His thumb skimmed under the top of her shorts, stayed there, and I knew I needed to leave before I ended killing the sonofabitch.

"I'm out of here," I told my brother without looking in his direction. My gaze was locked on Jos, and from the tilt of her lips in that smug little smile, I knew she could feel me watching her. This was all a show, one for my benefit. "This place is a total sausage fest anyway. I'm going home. Got shit to do in the morning."

"I'm headed to the clubhouse," Matt told me. "Pay the tab."

Muttering a curse, I pulled out my wallet as I walked toward the bar where Colt was washing glasses.

As I drew closer, Jos turned her head, her eyes rolling over me. The guy said something close to her ear and she bit her lip, but I could read everything she was thinking—and her thoughts weren't on the little pussy-assed bitch standing in her personal space. I saw a flash of the hurt I'd already inflicted the week before, along with the same, never-ending hunger that lived inside of me like a parasite.

I clenched my fingers around the bills in my hand and tried to pull my eyes away from Jos as I reached the bar. Unsuccessfully.

"You leaving?" Colt's voice didn't have the power to pull my gaze from the way Jos's eyes were begging me to come take her away from the guy she was with.

"Yeah," I muttered, dropping the cash on the bar top.

Colt followed my gaze. "Don't worry, I'm not letting her drink. She's just having a little fun."

"She's getting herself into trouble is what she's doing. She doesn't have to be drinking to do that."

Jos turned away, having heard what I'd just said, and pressed her hands to the guy's chest. One hand started playing with the buttons on his shirt, while the other slid south teasingly, her fingertips tracing over the obvious hard-on in the guy's jeans.

Mine.

A red haze washed over my eyes, and I was at the other end of the bar before I could even draw another breath. Grabbing her hand in a tight hold, I jerked her away from her friend and started dragging her toward the door.

"She's with me, asshole," the guy yelled behind us.

"Fuck off. I'm taking her home before she gets herself in trouble."

"I don't want to go home," Jos said with a pout as I slammed through the door and out into the parking lot, stomping toward my bike. At least she wasn't putting up a struggle, telling me she was getting exactly what she wanted from me.

"Too fucking bad," I snarled, stopping only when we reached the motorcycle, and I thrust my helmet into her hands. "Get on the fucking bike, Jos."

I tossed my leg over, waiting for her to climb on behind me. Without hesitating, she did, her arms locking around my abdomen, her cheek pressed to my back.

And just like that, most of the rage clouding my vision dissipated.

It left me feeling weak—and hard as fuck. I wanted her so goddamn bad I couldn't breathe without it physically hurting.

Now what the fuck am I going to do?

I needed to take her home. Pound on Butch's door until he opened up and promised me he wouldn't let his little girl out of the house again until she was fifty.

That was the rational thing to do. The one that wouldn't let me commit more sins than I already had with this female. But my cock was drilling into my zipper, begging for freedom. The feel of her hands on my stomach, her fingers sliding under my T-shirt and skimming along the top of my jeans, was driving me fucking crazy.

One more night.

That was all I needed. Just one more night and then I'd send her packing.

CHAPTER TEN

TANNER

I didn't bother flipping the lights on as I guided Jos through the quiet house in the direction of my bedroom.

Her skin felt hot to the touch as I kept my hands on her waist, my lips already on her neck as we climbed the stairs. She tasted so damn good, I could have licked her skin all night and still not gotten my fill of her. Her hips rolled back against me, torturing me with the tease of her ass rubbing my cock through my jeans.

"Jos, you mean little bitch," I groaned at her ear. "Stop before I fuck you right here in the hall."

"I'm okay with that." She tossed over her shoulder, her voice on the verge of breathlessness.

"Fuck this." Lifting her, I practically sprinted the last bit to my room and kicked the door shut before laying her on the bed and following her down.

My cut disappeared along with my T-shirt. Her top was out of my way, and her bra sailed over my shoulder as I unsnapped her pathetic excuse for shorts and plunged my hand inside, feeling how wet she was for me.

"Mmm," she moaned, licking her lips, her eyes closing in pleasure. "I've wanted this all week."

I pushed the shorts and panties out of my way, spreading her wide so I could put my mouth on her sweet little cunt. It was wrong. She'd just turned eighteen a few weeks before, but fuck, I wanted her so goddamn bad.

She screamed my name when I sucked her drenched pussy lips into my mouth before licking her from her opening all the way up to her clit. She thrust her fingers into my hair, clutching me to her.

"Tanner...ah, fuck. That feels so good. Please don't stop."

Within a minute, I had her begging me to finish her, to fuck her. I stood, the last of my viable brain cells shouting to glove it up before I sank balls deep into her. Cursing, I pulled open the nightstand drawer where I kept my condoms. Kissing my way up her body, I grasped the foil packet, tearing it open without ever lifting my lips from her sweetly delicious body.

When I reached her tits, I sucked her nipples until she was writhing underneath me, then sat back on my heels as I rolled the rubber down over my cock.

Looking down at her, I had to take a second to catch my breath. The need in her eyes made them glassy. The pink in her cheeks drove me crazy but not nearly as much as the sight of the love bites I'd left on her tits and her stomach. Seeing the gloss of wetness on her thighs, I couldn't have waited another second even if there had been a gun pointed at my head.

Spreading her legs wider, I sank slowly into her tightness. Each inch I fed into her was sweet agony, her pussy walls a contradiction, trying to push me out yet suck me deeper. Those little sounds she was making as I gave her what she wanted only amped up my raging need for her.

"Tanner," she moaned, her nails biting into my thighs as she looked between us, watching as I made us one entity. "Oh God, it feels so good."

"Don't move," I growled when she shifted her hips, taking me deeper before I was ready. I was trying to take my time, wanting to savor every second of this night before I had to throw her out of my life—for both our sakes—in the morning. But the way she was moving was driving me closer to the edge, and I knew if she didn't stop, this was going to be over before I wanted it to be.

"Please," she begged, her hips lifting and falling as she fucked herself on my cock. "I need you to make me come."

I found her clit with my thumb, pressing down hard. I rubbed slow circles until she was shaking, sweat beading on my brow, dripping down my temple. Fuck, I was going to blow just feeling the way she was contracting around me as she fought her orgasm.

"Jos, baby, I don't want to come yet." I pulled out, and she whimpered like she was in physical pain. "Shh, shh," I soothed, turning her on her side and lying down behind her. I pulled her ass closer, pressing on the small of her back just enough to angle her so I could take her from behind. "I'll give you what you want, sweetheart. Just trying to make this last as long as I can for myself."

I was only halfway in her like this. It was a tease, but it wasn't making me ready to nut off yet. She took one of my hands from her waist, lifting it to her tit. Her fingers cupped around mine, urging me to squeeze. I kissed her neck, her shoulder, then down her back, producing goose bumps everywhere my lips grazed.

The hand playing with her tit rubbed lower, stroking up and down her flat stomach before sliding between her legs to play with her clit. A mewl-like sound left her as I flicked my thumb over the very top of the little bundle of nerves. Her pussy walls contracted around me as more moisture flooded her channel, and each thrust turned the room into an erotic soundtrack to our fucking.

She came for the second time with me playing with her clit, and I had to pull free or risk coming then and there. I turned her to face me even as she was trying to float down from her second release. Lifting her leg, I pulled her thigh over mine and drove back into her.

Her hands clutched at my arms, her head tipped back and giving me the perfect access to feast on her neck. I marked her as mine with little love bites from her ear to her shoulder as I took my time pumping into her. I stroked my fingers up her leg then down her hips, teasing at her ass crack. She shivered, moaning her encouragement as I let my thumb linger on her tiny little asshole.

"You like that?" I groaned against her neck. "You want me to play with you here?"

"I-I don't know," she breathed, but her ass pressed back into my touch, telling me she wanted it but was afraid of asking for it.

I dipped my fingers down, touching my cock as it entered her, scooping up the thick wetness on my shaft before plunging into her again and again. When my index finger was soaked, I returned to that little hole she was so unsure of.

My finger teased her at first, seeing how far she really did want me to go. When I stuck the very tip inside her hole, she let out a surprised little squeal, but her pussy contracted around my cock as she started to come for the third time. I finger-fucked her hole through her release, but as soon as she was able to lift her eyes again, I was lost. I grabbed her hips in both hands and rolled us so that I was on top of her, and I fucked her hard until I was bellowing her name to the heavens.

***

A moan coming from Jos had me squinting my eyes open hours later. She was lying half on top of me, her face pressed into my chest. She was still asleep, but I could feel how wet she was as her pussy pressed down on my thigh.

"Fuck, baby," I groaned and lifted her hips until she could slide down onto my cock.

Her eyes drifted open when I entered her, and she smiled down at me sleepily. "I like waking up from a dream of you fucking me, to you actually fucking me."

I laughed, making my chest vibrate against her tits. "I like it a little too."

I fucking loved it. I wanted to do this every damn night, but I knew it would never happen. As soon as my alarm went off for me to get up for work, I was going to have to end this once and for all.

She sat up, steadying herself by putting her hands on my stomach. It was the first time she'd ever been on top, but she didn't seem unsure of herself. Instead, she moved her hips like she'd been doing this all her damn life, and it drove me crazy.

"Oh God, this feels so good," she whimpered.

I sat up, holding her hips so she wouldn't fall backward, letting her ride me but able to bury my face in between her tits now. Sucking one nipple into my mouth roughly, I groaned against her flesh as her inner walls contracted around my rock-hard cock.

"Tanner," she breathed, her hands clutching at my shoulders like I was the only thing anchoring her to the earth. "Could...Could you do that thing again? With your finger and my...my..."

Grinning around her nipple, I brushed my thumb over her little asshole, and she began to shudder as her release hit her hard.

"Ah, God!" she screamed, falling forward weakly.

Holding on to her, I scooted us to the end of the bed. Pulling free from her, I turned her on my lap, and her feet hit the floor a little drunkenly. Brushing her hair out of the way, I sucked on her shoulder, marking her as mine yet again. "Tease me, Jos," I urged.

"H-How?"

I spread her ass cheeks and pulled her back so that my shaft fit along the seam. I guided her up and down, showing her how to tease me by rubbing that sweet ass over my cock.

"Shit, that feels good," she moaned.

I let her tease me, no longer guiding her movements but holding her cheeks spread apart so I could watch. My tip leaked jizz, coating her skin with the thick liquid. She was killing me, but I would die a happy man.

"Tanner," she whined suddenly. "I need you again. Now."

"Hell," I grunted and flipped her facedown on the bed. I plunged balls deep into her pussy, lost, mindless to everything but making her come and feeling that tight little cunt squeezing around my cock so hard when she did.

***

It was a long while later before I could breathe again.

We were both coated in sweat, and the entire room smelled like the wild sex we'd just had. It was a heady scent that made me punch-drunk. Or maybe that was just because I'd come harder than I could ever remember coming in my entire life.

Sweet little Jos was untamable in bed, my perfect match, and I was pretty sure I was going to die when she left me.

A glance at the digital clock on the side table told me my alarm was going to go off in just a few short minutes. Despite the sweat still beading on my brow, I suddenly felt chilled to my bones, and my arms unconsciously contracted around Jos. She gave a little mewl of protest, shifting in my arms, and I instantly released her.

Pushing her thigh off my leg, I sat up, reaching for my phone.

"Are you going to work today?" she asked sleepily. "You could call in sick. I'll make sure Grandpa won't fire you if you stay in bed with me all day."

That offer was so tempting, but I knew I couldn't take her up on it. If I didn't do this now, I wasn't ever going to be able to bring myself to, and she deserved so much more than what I could give her.

"I'm thinking about taking the day off," I told her as I sent the text and stood. I tossed my phone carelessly on the bed, knowing she would be able to see it. "But I'm a little bored with you now. Thought maybe I would get a little variety. Someone with some actual skills to come over and finish what you couldn't."

Her small gasp crushed my soul, but I didn't stop on my way to the door.

"Are you joking?" she demanded, her voice choked. "Tanner? Tanner! Come back here and tell me you're joking."

"Sorry, sweetheart. I need a shower. It's not polite to have a girl's cream on your cock when you're expecting someone else."

"What? Why are you doing this?"

Halfway through the doorway, I turned and looked back. It was hard to keep my expression blank when I saw the tears in her eyes, but I reminded myself I was doing this for her. "Last night was fun, but it took for-fucking-ever for you to get me off. I need someone who knows what she's doing. You can stick around and watch if you want, maybe learn a few things. If you do, we can try this again tonight."

She jerked up out of bed, her face pale, her eyes blazing. "How can you say that to me? I thought... I just... I don't understand," she whispered, her voice breaking.

I hardened my heart, forcing myself to meet her gaze. "Plain and simple, Jos. You're not what I want. The only reason I brought you home with me last night was because you were pissing me the fuck off. It took everything in me to even nut off last night. You can't satisfy me. You're too green, and I need women with experience."

"You sonofabitch!" she cried. "You weren't saying that last night when you kept telling me you didn't want to come too fast. That you wanted it to last."

I shrugged. "I just said that so you wouldn't feel bad that I wasn't getting off."

Tears filled her eyes, but she picked up the first thing she could get her hands on—my alarm clock—and threw it at my head. I ducked backward just as it crashed into the doorframe and exploded into three large pieces.

"I thought last night was special, you motherfucking asshole!" she screamed, picking up something else to throw. She picked up an empty beer bottle I'd left there recently. I ducked down, and it hit the hall wall, shattering at my feet. "I love your dumb ass, and you're treating me like this? Do you even like me, you goddamn prick?"

"You're cute, but spoiled," I told her, hating myself for doing this to her. "All you want is your own way, and I gave it to you after you shook your ass at me all week. Why are you throwing a tantrum after getting what you wanted, Jos?"

"What I wanted?" she repeated, the tears falling unchecked from her eyes. "You think this was what I wanted? For you to fuck me all night and then break my heart the next morning?"

"Sorry if I'm breaking your heart," I told her. "I thought you knew the score. This is why I don't get involved with anyone younger than me. You young chicks get too clingy. It's just about sex, sweetheart. No offense, babe, but no experience and following a guy around like a lost puppy is a huge turn-off for me."

I'm so fucking sorry. I want you. I love you. I fucking need you. Don't hate me. Don't leave me.

But I didn't speak those words aloud, didn't let her see them as they roared through my head. I stood there, my heart racing as she rushed to get dressed and then stomped out of my bedroom.

As she passed me, she stopped, her hand flying out and slapping me hard across the face. I didn't even flinch, just welcomed the pain. It couldn't equal the pain I was inflicting on her—as well as myself.

"You're such a fucking coward, Tanner Reid. I don't know what I saw in you that made me love you, but as soon as I find out, I'm burning it out of my system."

CHAPTER ELEVEN

TANNER

Present Day

Jos shifted in her sleep, her brows puckered. I traced my index finger over them, and she sighed again, leaning forward into my touch.

"Reid," she breathed. "Reid?" She jerked upright, looking around the room dazedly. "Reid?"

"Sorry, sweetheart. I'm the only Reid present."

She squeezed the back of her neck with one hand as she fell back against the plastic chair she was sitting in. "I couldn't find him," she muttered. "No one could tell me where he was."

My gut clenched. "You named our son Reid?"

"It was the only way I thought he would ever have your last name," she said, her shoulders lifting in a small shrug.

I was glad the head of the bed was lifted so I didn't have to look up at her. It seemed surreal just to be talking to her. That we were discussing her son—our son—blew my mind. I'd never thought about having kids. Lexa, Max, and whatever kids Matt ended up having could carry on our last name.

I was a father.

I was responsible for a little life I didn't even know existed.

Maybe I should have been pissed Jos kept him from me, but considering how badly I'd treated her that last morning, I was pretty sure I deserved it.

"Do you have a picture?" I asked, my hands oddly sweaty.

Her lashes lifted, revealing surprised eyes, but she pulled her phone from her jeans pocket and swiped her thumb over the screen a few times before offering it to me. "I took these last night while the boys were eating," she said as my eyes landed on a picture of two little boys sitting in identical high chairs feeding each other spaghetti.

I swiped through her collection of pictures, all of which were of my son. I traced his image with my thumb. There was no denying this kid was mine. He looked just like me, with the exception of those curls. That was all I could see of his mother in him until I found a picture of him smiling. The way his lips lifted reminded me of Jos.

The next picture was a selfie of mother and son, and my heart turned over. "Will you print this picture off for me?" I asked her, unable to tear my gaze from the picture of Reid's face squished to his mother's cheek, giving her a sloppy kiss. The look on her face was full of love, reminding me of our very first night together and the way she'd looked up at me after I'd taken her virginity.

"Um, yeah, sure. If you really want me to."

I nodded and finally looked up from the screen. "I would really appreciate it, Jos."

Her frown deepened. "Are you feeling okay?"

Handing her back the phone, I didn't answer. "They're doing my surgery today?"

Sliding the phone into her pocket, she nodded. "I spoke to Doc last night. They can still do the surgery this morning, but he wasn't sure what time. Actually, the ortho surgeon here is better than the one in Eureka. He's more experienced and better qualified. Maybe you won't need a second surgery."

"Yeah, that's good." I closed my eyes, feeling the effects of the long ride from Eureka to Creswell Springs the night before. I was so damn tired, but at least my pain was completely manageable with the pain meds now.

"Aggie was talking about making all your favorite foods last night. So as soon as you feel up to eating, just let me know, and I'll tell her to get started on it."

Thinking of all the food I would have killed to eat right then, my stomach grumbled. "Tomorrow," I told her, rubbing my four-fingered hand over my abdomen. "They told me last night I couldn't have anything to eat or drink until after my surgery."

"Okay, tomorrow. Anything you want, I'll get them to make it."

"I can't have what I really want," I muttered, looking straight at her. Her cheeks filled with pink, and I began to relax. "Come here." Holding out my hand to her, I held my breath, waiting to see if she would take it.

For the span of two heartbeats, she hesitated, before taking my hand and letting me tug her into bed beside me. Everything inside of me suddenly felt at peace, and I carefully shifted onto my side, not paying any attention to the pain in my back at the movement. Her arm went around my waist, her forehead pressing into my chest. I cupped her ass, squeezing it gently.

"Don't run away from me again," I pleaded, my voice low and rough.

She blew out a heavy exhale but nodded. "Okay."

"I won't flirt with anyone but you from here on out. I'm sorry if it hurt you."

"Tanner—"

I kissed the top of her head. "I'm sorry I was a dick to you two years ago. I didn't mean anything I said that morning."

"Then why did you say it?" she whispered.

"Because I was an idiot."

A soft snort left her. "True."

I smacked her on the ass, making her squeal, then giggle. The sound filled my soul, and I grinned down at her when she tipped her head back to look up at me. "I kind of have a thing for you, Jos."

Her eyes darkened. "I've kind of always had a thing for you, Tanner."

I lowered my head, kissing the corner of her mouth. "Will you give us a chance to see what this thing is?" I already knew what this thing was. I loved this woman with every cell in my body. But I needed time to show her that.

"Are you sure you want to?" she asked hesitantly.

"Never been surer of anything in my life, baby." I skimmed my nose against hers, my breath teasing across her lips. "I've missed you so fucking much the last two years. Nearly dying showed me that I want to at least have the chance to build a future with you."

Her lashes lowered, and she inhaled slowly before blowing her breath out in a huff. When her eyes met mine again, she smiled. "Okay. We can try to see what this 'thing' between us is and where it could go." She leaned in, her fingers cupping my chin. "But I swear on all that is holy, Tanner Reid, if you break my heart, I'll gut you."

Heart full, I grinned down at her before kissing her.

A tap on the door pulled us apart, and I glanced over at the entrance to the private room. Doc didn't think I needed to be in ICU now, but he warned I might end up back there for a little while if my body didn't handle the surgery well for my arm.

I kept my good arm wrapped around Jos as the door cracked open, and Raider stuck his head inside. "Hey, Bates is being a little pissant. He wants to talk to you and take a statement. You up for that, or do you want me to sic Gracie on him?"

The air in my lungs turned to ice, and my hand clenched into a fist on Jos's back, instinctively pulling her in close.

Bates.

I'd forgotten about that motherfucker.

"Get in here and lock the goddamn door!" I yelled.

Raider didn't question me. He moved so he was inside the room with us and used his back to hold the door shut since there wasn't a damn lock.

"What the hell, Tanner?" Jos squeaked when I sat up, looking around frantically for somewhere to hide her.

"Something wrong, brother?" Raider asked, his voice calm as he watched me from across the room.

"Bates is the one who took me to Fontana," I whisper-shouted. "Help me hide Jos before that bastard sees her."

"Bates?" Raider's entire face changed, and he pulled his gun from the holster hidden under his cut. "That motherfucker did this to you?"

"Hide Jos!" I roared when he started to open the door.

"He's already fucking seen her," Raider yelled back. "He's been sniffing around the clubhouse for the past few weeks. He's seen her plenty of times."

"Goddamn it," I groaned. "Are you the only one here? Please tell me there are other brothers in the waiting room somewhere."

"Jet is talking to Bates at the nurses station. Colt is getting us some coffee, and Spider is watching the lobby," he assured me.

"The sheriff helped do this to you?" Jos breathed out raggedly. "He helped that monster hurt you?"

"The bomb blast threw me between two cars and knocked me out," I explained. "The next thing I knew, I was in some trunk. I passed out again from pain and then woke up to Bates and Fontana standing over me. He only stayed the first day. The rest was Fontana."

"He's a dead man," Raider seethed.

"You can't kill a cop." Jos tried to rationalize. "Not somewhere there is an entire building full of witnesses."

I almost grinned down at her. The fire burning in her eyes and making her shake was a hell of a turn-on, but I was too scared of Bates snatching her from me and taking her to Fontana. "You have to get out of here," I told her, pushing her legs off the bed and urging her to stand. "Raider will take you back to the compound. Bates can't see you with me."

She stood but glared down at me. "I'm not leaving until after your surgery."

"Jos, please," I begged her unashamedly. "Fontana knows you're the only thing that could even begin to crack me. He will use you to get to me, and Bates is his little bitch."

She grasped my four-fingered hand, squeezing lightly. "Calm down. Give me a second to think. Okay?"

"Baby—"

She covered my mouth with one hand. "Be quiet, Tanner. I'm thinking."

CHAPTER TWELVE

It was amusing to watch Jos boss Tanner around. At first, I didn't know what to make of those two together, but I could see now that Jos was what he needed.

She dropped her hand from his mouth and turned to face me. "Here's what we're going to do for now. Tanner is going to pretend he doesn't remember anything from when he was at Fontana's. Nothing. Don't even open your mouth, Tanner. Do you hear me?"

"What the fuck are you doing, Joslyn?" he growled low. "Get the fuck out of here before he sees you."

"You don't remember, do you understand?"

"What's that going to—"

"If you remember nothing, you're not a threat to him at the moment. Just play along until you guys can think of a better plan and take that piece of shit out." She pushed him back against the mattress and pulled the covers up to his chest. "Act like you're weak. Moans and groans are all that need to leave your mouth."

Her eyes landed on me. "Put the gun away, dumbass."

Fighting back a grin, I replaced my gun in the holster under my cut. "Yes, ma'am."

"Check to see if Jet is still talking to the sheriff. Tell him to come on in if he wants, but that Tanner isn't in any shape to make a statement."

"Jos, leave before he sees you," Tanner persisted, his eyes wild with panic.

"Relax," she commanded, making her sound just like Raven.

I opened the door and looked down the corridor to where the nurses station was. My oldest brother was still standing there talking to Bates, his face tight with annoyance. The sheriff had his back to me, but I could tell by the set of his shoulders he wasn't happy.

Jet caught my gaze, and I motioned to send the dirty pig back. With a single nod, he said something to Bates that had him turning in my direction.

Every instinct I had was screaming at me to pull my gun and put a bullet in that sonofabitch's brain. Three weeks of grief over thinking we'd lost Tanner. Three weeks of my MC brother being tortured. All of that could have been avoided if it weren't for this piece of shit.

"Is he coming?" Jos whispered from right behind me.

"On his way," I told her as I stepped back in and closed the door. "What's your plan, Jos? I need to know so I don't fuck anything up."

"Just pretend you don't know anything. Tanner has been so sick, he can barely talk. Act normal. I'm sure you and the other MC brothers will come up with some way to take Bates out, but this will give you some wiggle room so none of you end up on death row for killing a cop in front of witnesses."

I liked that she wasn't blind to the fact that Bates needed to die. If anything, the rage simmering in her eyes told me she would have liked to put a bullet or two in the man herself.

"You're going to have to watch your back until Bates is taken out," I advised, keeping my voice low so no one outside the room would hear.

"I'll worry about that later."

The door opened without warning, and Bates sauntered in like he owned the place, Jet right behind him. Bates's jowly face seemed stressed as his beady eyes swept over the room and landed on Tanner.

A pitiful moan left my MC brother, his eyelids fluttering as he shifted on the bed. "Jos," he groaned. "Is someone else here?"

She went back to his side, gently touching his brow. "It's just the sheriff, honey. Are you up to talking to him?"

"Not really," he sighed tiredly.

"I won't take up much of your time," Bates said, sounding concerned.

"He really isn't up for talking, Sheriff," Jos told him, her lips pressed into a sad, grim line. Tears filled her eyes. "He's not even coherent most of the time. I've tried to get him to tell me what happened, but he doesn't seem to remember anything."

Jet nudged me from my left, his brows lifted. I gave a quick shake of my head, telling him to keep quiet.

"I still need to speak to him, Miss Barker. The sooner I can get a statement, the quicker I can wrap up the investigation."

Two fat tears fell from Jos's eyes, and she sniffled. "I understand. But please be brief."

Bates moved closer to the bed, and I had to clench my hands into fists to keep from grabbing him and throwing him out the window.

He crossed to the same side of the bed where Jos was standing, and I could almost feel the tension coming off Tanner. She leaned down and kissed his cheek, and he began to relax a little. "Honey, just try to talk to the sheriff."

"Reid, we thought you died in the bomb that went off in your brother's truck. We have a death certificate for you. How is it you're alive?"

"I…" Tanner shook his head, frowning like he was in pain and trying to capture a memory that wouldn't come. "I don't know. I remember starting Matt's truck…then nothing."

"Where have you been all this time?"

"A spa in the California vineyards," Jet told him dryly. "Can't you tell it did him some good? His skin looks so refreshed."

Bates flipped him off. "Reid?"

"I don't know," Tanner muttered weakly. "It's all blank."

"The doctor said you were in a hospital in Eureka. That's where you were?"

"I don't know," Tanner repeated, closing his eyes. "My head hurts, Jos. It hurts so bad."

She stroked her hand over his face still in need of a shave. "I'm sorry, sweetie. The sheriff will just have to wait." She lifted her head to give the sheriff the look I saw Raven give anyone who displeased her. It wasn't as fierce as my sister's, but it did the trick. "Sheriff Bates, I'm sorry, but this will have to wait, after all. Tanner has a skull fracture. Doc thinks he might have amnesia. Maybe once the swelling has gone down, he will remember something that could help you."

"Right," Bates muttered, but he was more relaxed than he had been when he'd first walked into the room. "I'll be back in a few days, then. Keep me posted if he does remember something so we can get his statement."

Jos nodded solemnly. "Of course. I'll make sure you're the first to know." She walked with him to the door. "I really appreciate you coming, Sheriff. I can relax a little knowing you're trying to protect Tanner. He's so weak right now. When he was in Eureka, he coded twice, and we nearly lost him. I hope you catch the monster who did this to him."

"Just doing my job, ma'am." He gave her a stiff nod and headed for the elevators.

She stood there, watching until he got on, then closed the door. Leaning back against it, she let out a small shriek of anger. "That smarmy motherfucker," she hissed.

"Care to tell me what the hell was going on with that little performance?" Jet demanded, glaring at all three of us. "If I didn't know better, I swear I would have thought Tanner was close to death again."

I gave my brother a brief summary of what had happened, and I had to grab his shoulders to keep him from running after Bates. It wasn't all that long ago that Jet had been on parole after going to prison for manslaughter. There would be no saving him if someone saw him killing Bates. I couldn't lose my brother again. Couldn't let Flick and Raven lose him again.

"Calm down. We'll take care of Bates," I promised him. "But we've got to do this smart. Jos bought us some time, so let's use it. Call Bash. And maybe Gracie too. She needs to know what Bates did."

While Jet tried to calm himself enough to make the calls, a nurse came in to check on Tanner. She took his vitals, said the surgeon would be in to speak to him soon, and then left with the promise of more pain medication.

By the time the doctor came in to talk to Tanner about the surgery they were going to perform on his arm, Colt and Spider had joined us, and Bash was walking through the door with Hawk and Gracie.

Gracie's brows lifted as soon as she saw me standing there. "You're still here?"

"Where else would I be...? Fuck!" Stabbing my fingers into my hair, I groaned and pulled out my phone as I sprinted out the door.

It rang and rang until, finally, Quinn picked up. "I'm about to walk into the doctor's office," she said, not sounding mad like I was hoping. But from her tone, I knew she was disappointed. "Little John drove me since I know how much you hate me leaving the clubhouse by myself. I waited for you and even tried to call, but I guess you have bad service in the hospital."

"Baby, I'm on my way." The damn elevator was taking too long, so I took the stairs, running like my life depended on it. "Something came up with Tanner and..." And I forgot. Fuck. I was the worst. Quinn was always on my mind, always, but this shit with Tanner had pushed everything to the side. Including my pregnant fiancée.

"I understand," she said softly, but I still heard the hurt.

"I'll be there in two minutes, I swear." I hit the lobby, still running. "I love you. I'll see you soon."

Luckily for me, her OB-GYN was in the same medical complex as the hospital. I ran across the parking lot to the medical facility, cursing my sorry ass the entire time.

Sweat dripped down my back as I opened the door to her doctor's office and nearly collided with her. Eyes wide, she stepped back so I didn't send her crashing to the floor. "Are the hounds of hell chasing you?"

"Yeah, baby. And they want to drag me down for forgetting about your doctor's appointment." I grasped her waist in both hands and pulled her in close, kissing her softly. When I lifted my head, she leaned against me weakly. My kisses always made her weak-kneed, and I prayed that never changed. "I'm sorry."

Her smile lit up my heart. "I forgive you. This time. Next time, I might kick you in the balls, though."

"I take it you only want this one kid, then?"

She gave me a sassy grin. "Who said you were going to be my only baby daddy?"

Jealousy and possessiveness turned my vision red, my fingers contracting on her waist until she squirmed in protest. "Take it back," I growled, kissing her again. "Take it back right now."

That sassy grin didn't falter as she pulled back and went to sit down in one of the few vacant chairs. It was only then that I realized the place was packed and everyone was watching us like we were some soap opera they were enthralled by.

"Raider," Quinn called softly, amusement shining out of those blue eyes. "Sit down."

Crossing the waiting room, I sat beside her. She leaned forward, running her fingers through my hair to fix it. I took advantage of her closeness and kissed her. Pulling back, she slapped me playfully on the cheek. I caught her hand, noticing she still didn't have an engagement ring.

I needed to remedy that—and today.

Ten minutes passed before a nurse called Quinn's name. I walked back with her, waited outside the bathroom while she peed in a cup, then followed her into an exam room.

"Looks like you've lost a little weight," the nurse commented. "Is the morning sickness still holding on?"

"It comes and goes," Quinn said with a dismissive shrug.

"Just stay hydrated. Don't worry about eating if you don't feel up to it." She took Quinn's vitals, made a notation, then left us to wait for the doctor.

Quinn sat on the exam table, her short legs swinging back and forth as she looked around the room at all the different posters on the walls. One was a flyer reminding parents to sign up for the Lamaze classes early because they filled up quick.

I pulled out my phone and started to text the number to sign us up.

"I already did that," Quinn said, stopping me. "On my first visit."

"So I'm signed up as your partner?"

Her teeth sank into her bottom lip for a second before she shook her head. "At the time, I didn't know who would end up being my partner, so I just left that blank. Actually, I don't even know why I signed up. I was still planning on leaving."

My gut clenched, and I had to force myself to relax. She wasn't leaving. She was mine now, and she was going to marry me. Soon. I wasn't sure how long I could wait to have her marked with my last name, knowing she was mine forever.

"How fast do you think we can plan a wedding?" I asked her, leaning back against the wall near the door.

She frowned. "I don't know. A few months, at least. Raven's took what—six months?"

"That's too long to wait. I was thinking more like a few weeks."

"Yeah, okay," she snorted, rolling her eyes at me. "What's with you? Why are you in such a rush? I thought we would wait until after the baby was born."

"Not happening," I told her point-blank. "I want my rings on your finger, you sharing my last name, and legally bound to me before this kid is born."

"I repeat, why the rush?" she asked, tilting her head to the side, studying me.

"The rush is we don't know what tomorrow brings." I pushed away from the wall and crossed to her. She spread her legs as I moved between them, cupping my hands around her throat and using my thumbs to tilt her head back so our gazes locked. "I want you as my wife. Now, not tomorrow. I want the world to know that... You. Are. Mine."

Love flashed in her eyes, and she wrapped her legs around my waist, locking me in place. "I know that I'm yours. Isn't that enough?"

"Have you seen how beautiful you are?" I demanded incredulously. "Woman, every man looks at you and wants you for himself. I'm the lucky sonofabitch who has you, and I want to make sure they fucking know it."

Her laugh was soft and precious. "And if I said I want you to wear a ring so the whole world—and more importantly, every woman alive—knows you are taken?"

"Baby, I'm tattooing a ring around this finger with your name. I'll wear whatever the hell you want me to wear, and if any other woman even looks at me, I'll tell her I married the most beautiful, amazing, sweetest girl in the universe." I brushed my lips over hers, felt her soft gasp of air as it brushed over my mouth. "Marry me soon, Quinn. Please, I'm begging. Don't make me wait."

She pressed her forehead into my chest, her fingers clinging to my cut. "Okay," she said without hesitation. "Let's make it happen."

CHAPTER THIRTEEN

After cleaning up my mess in the bathroom, I opened the door to the bedroom and glanced out. Matt was sound asleep on our bed, snoring like a bear in the middle of hibernation. The past week had taken its toll on him, and last night was the first time he'd slept more than an hour or two since they'd found Tanner.

Quietly, I left the bedroom, shutting the door on my way out.

Wiping the sweat off my brow from having just spent the last half hour throwing up everything in my stomach, I was exhausted, but there were things I needed to take care of.

In the kitchen, I found Raven and asked for the keys to her Challenger.

"You okay?" she asked as she readily handed over the key ring.

I met her gaze, let her see everything in my eyes, but I didn't say the words that wanted to trip off my tongue. Green eyes widened, and then she shook her head. "Something in the freaking water," she muttered.

"I don't know when I'll be back. Don't tell Matt where I'm going."

She shrugged. "I don't know where you are going, so no worries there. Just be careful. If it looks like someone other than a brother is following you, call me or Matt."

Driving into town, I left the window cracked, and I didn't miss the man on the motorcycle following me like a dark cloud over my head. But I refused to think about the constant babysitter I had whenever I so much as left the clubhouse compound.

The chilly breeze felt good on my flushed skin. First stop was the drugstore. I needed a pregnancy test, stat. Raven was right. There was definitely something in the water. If I was pregnant like I suspected, that would make four of us in the clubhouse who were expecting. Gracie and Willa both announced their pregnancies the previous week, and with Quinn pregnant too, at least I wouldn't have to go through all this crap alone.

I touched a hand to my stomach, unsure how I felt about being a mother this early into my relationship with Matt. If I were honest, I was still having issues with the three years we'd been apart. I'd thought I was okay with everything after we talked about him hooking up with Steph while I was gone. But then Joslyn showed up with her son, and I realized I wasn't nearly as over it as I kept telling myself I was.

Reid wasn't Matt's son, but it drove home to me just how easily he could have been. The man I loved hadn't been a monk while we were apart. He could have fucked any number of women during that time, and it was driving me crazy.

Was I ready to bring a baby into this relationship when everything was so up in the air with my feelings?

What if I couldn't get over this jealousy that ate at me just thinking of all the other women he'd had sex with?

"Pull your shit together, Michaels. Find out if you are or not before you go buying more trouble."

I walked into the drugstore and straight back to where the pregnancy tests and condoms were kept, grateful the MC brother waiting outside wouldn't be able to see exactly what I was about to buy. I grabbed the one that would give me a digital reading and headed for the checkout. Thankfully, the place had had a recent update, and there was a single self-checkout, which I took full advantage of instead of having the woman behind the counter know my business.

Tossing the test in a bag, I swiped my card, took my receipt, and stomped out.

As I walked through the automatic door, however, someone was walking in. Catching his gaze on me, I clenched my hands on my bag, glad the gray plastic would hide the contents as I glared up at my father.

Dressed in one of his thousand-dollar suits, his hair slicked back, and his face glowing from a recent facial, no doubt, he looked like the politician he was. His bid for governor had already been announced, and it was only a matter of time before he started campaigning. He just needed me to release the money I'd promised to start the ball rolling.

"Hello, Aurora," he greeted with a tight smile.

"Dad," I bit out and kept walking.

"It's good to see you," he called after me.

"Can't say the same," I said as I jerked open the car door.

Tossing the bag into the passenger seat, I got in and locked the doors before starting the vehicle. Ten minutes later, I pulled up outside of Jenkins's office. As I walked in, Jenkins was coming out of his office, as if he were expecting me.

"You didn't have to come in," he said by way of greeting. "I could have brought the contract and release papers out to you."

I shrugged. "I was already out. Might as well get this over with."

Something in my tone had his eyes widening, and I quickly pushed down everything else that was bothering me. One thing at a time. I would deal with this first, officially shutting my father out of my life and the MC's business, and then I would conquer the other shit on my never-ending list.

"Come on back," Jenkins urged, and I followed him to his office. "Gracie already drew up everything, but she's out of the office this morning. She said she had to go to the hospital for Tanner. How is he doing?"

"Matt said he's lucky to be alive." I didn't know how much to tell the lawyer, so I kept it at that. I wasn't even sure I knew everything. Matt hadn't talked to me much the last week, and I'd been a little distant to him ever since Jos and Reid arrived. "It surprised everyone when we found out Tanner didn't die from the bomb that was in Matt's truck."

I was still trying to wrap my mind around the fact that he was alive. I was so happy to have him back, not just for Matt's sake, but because I loved Tanner like a brother. He never treated me like an outsider, always put me at ease, and joked with me. I wanted to visit him at the hospital, but Matt asked me to wait until later in the week, after his brother had gotten through the surgery to fix his broken arm. They didn't want to overwhelm him with too many visitors at once, I guess.

That didn't sting at all, though.

Not one little bit.

It was okay. Matt pushing me back, keeping me on the sidelines was fine.

The sarcasm of my inner voice was giving me a damn headache.

"Let's see," Jenkins muttered as he shifted a few files on his desk. "Here it is."

He passed over the paper to me that released my inheritance. I traced my fingertips over my mother's name, and I wished she were there with me. All that money, but it wasn't enough to save her or bring her back. I needed her guidance so desperately right then. How was I going to deal with being pregnant if I really was? What if I fucked up being a mother?

Why did she have to die before I was ready to face the reality of the world without her?

"If you're not ready, we don't have to do this today," Jenkins assured me in a quiet voice.

"N-No," I told him with a trembling smile. "I'd rather just be done with it all."

Taking the pen he offered, I scribbled my name across the bottom of the release form and handed it back to him. Next came the contract detailing the deal I'd made my father. I read it over, saw that everything we'd discussed was there, and then signed my name on the line under my father, who had already signed the night I'd made the offer.

Once it was done, I felt a little of the pressure that was weighing down my shoulders release.

"You have your grandparents' house and a little over a million dollars that is still yours," the lawyer reminded me. "Should I release that to your personal bank account, or would you like me to be responsible for investing it for you?"

I pressed my fingers to my temples where a headache was starting to throb. "I want half to go into my personal account. The other half, I want to go into a trust fund for any children I have."

He made a notation. "And the house? I can have it sold for you. It's worth a good bit of money."

"No, not yet," I advised him. "Let me think about it for a bit. I don't know what I want to do with it just yet."

"Your choice. Just let me know." He smiled warmly. "Is there anything else you need me to take care of?"

I shook my head, trying to relax a little. "The special election is next week. Are you ready?"

Since my father had resigned as mayor to put in his bid for governor, the town was having a special election to replace him. Jenkins was running, and there was only one other opponent— Royce Campbell, the current DA.

But since Campbell was running for mayor, he'd had to resign from his position as DA as well. His assistant had stepped into his place, which was a good thing, from all the talk I'd heard lately. Rita

Sheppard was a ballbuster but under no one's control, unlike Campbell, who'd always been my father's little bitch lackey.

It was going to be a close election, though, but I knew who I was voting for. If Jenkins won, however, that meant Gracie would have to step into his shoes completely.

"I'll be glad once it's all over," Jenkins told me with a tired laugh. "This crap is exhausting."

"Creswell Springs will be a better place with you as our mayor," I assured him. "We need you."

"I guess we'll have to see how many people think the same way. Just make sure you vote on Tuesday."

The sound of my phone had me pulling it out of my purse. Seeing the name on the screen, I quickly said goodbye to Jenkins and walked out of the office before answering. I unlocked the car as I lifted the phone to my ear.

"Where are you?" Matt demanded.

"I'm on my way back now," I assured him. "I had a few errands to run."

"Like?"

"Jenkins needed me to finalize my inheritance distribution. Dad is officially out of our hair once and for all." I started the Challenger. Putting the phone on speaker, I tossed it into the cupholder then backed out of the parking space.

"Are you okay?" he asked, his voice softening.

I shifted gears and headed for the clubhouse, once again seeing the motorcycle and its rider in the rearview mirror. "I'm good now that I know Derrick Michaels can't ever bother you again."

"You should have woken me up," he grumbled. "I would have taken you."

"I wanted you to sleep. You haven't slept in an actual bed in over a week." *And I didn't want you to know what I was buying earlier,* I thought to myself.

"I'm getting ready to head back to the hospital. Tanner's surgery is in an hour. Do you want to meet me over there?"

I sucked my bottom lip between my teeth, hesitating. "I thought you wanted me to wait until after his surgery before I came over."

"I changed my mind. Meet me there, okay?"

"Yeah," I told him, turning at the next stop sign so I could head over to the hospital. "I'll see you soon."

"Be careful, baby. I love you."

I clenched my eyes shut for a moment before opening them again to focus on the road. "I love you too."

CHAPTER FOURTEEN

Raven's car was already in the parking lot when I got to the hospital, but Rory wasn't waiting on me. Instantly, my gut clenched and my heart started pounding. I jogged into the hospital lobby, looking for any sign of her even as I pulled out my phone.

It rang twice before she answered. "I'm in the bathroom. Stop freaking out," was her greeting. "Give me, like, two more minutes, okay?"

I let out a relieved breath. "Okay, baby. Take your time."

I found the women's bathroom and stood outside the door as I waited for her, scrolling through the group texts on my phone I'd missed earlier. There was one from Bash to all the MC brothers, letting us know to avoid Bates for the moment, and he would explain more during church later that night.

Nothing unusual about that. We were always avoiding Bates, but something about the text left me feeling uneasy.

The door to the bathroom opened, and Rory came out, still drying her hands with a paper towel. I took one look at her and knew something was wrong. Her face was pale, and there was sweat on her brow. Her eyes were unfocused as she stepped into the corridor, as if her mind was a million miles away.

When she realized I was standing right in front of her, she jumped in surprise. "You didn't have to wait for me," she said, her voice weak.

I took her hand and guided her down the hall to the chapel. Shutting the door behind us, I turned to face her. For some reason, I felt anxious just looking at her. Whatever was going on, I needed to fix it now. I knew something had been off with her since Jos arrived. The whole confrontation with Butch still hadn't been discussed because I'd been so fucking busy.

"Are you sick?" I asked, touching my thumb to her forehead and wiping away a smear of sweat.

"Just an upset stomach. Maybe I shouldn't be here, after all. I don't want to chance giving Tanner this stomach bug."

"Stomach bug," I repeated, shaking my head. There were enough pregnant women in the clubhouse for me to recognize the signs. A grin started to tease at my lips despite the shit we still needed to talk about. "Is it really a bug? Or did you catch something else?"

She looked away, and I had my answer.

My grin disappeared before it even fully formed. "Were you going to tell me?"

"I just found out, okay?" she snapped and walked toward the front of the chapel. Sitting down on the bench, she glared up at the cross on the wall. "I took a test while I was in the bathroom. I'm still trying to process it."

"What's there to process?" I asked, crouching down in front of her. "We're going to have a baby. I'm pretty damn happy."

"Well, I'm not," she whispered, tears spilling over her lashes. "I don't know how to be a mother. I don't know how to deal with this jealousy that is eating at me. And I can't fucking breathe right now."

My heart stopped, watching her struggle. "Don't say that," I choked out, more scared than I'd ever been in my life. "Rory, we'll figure it out."

She lowered her head, her hair falling into her face and effectively shutting me out. My fingers shook as I pushed it back, desperate to touch her. "Why are you so jealous? What happened to make you doubt me?"

"I don't doubt you," she answered, her lashes fluttering closed. "I know you love me. I know you're mine. I'm struggling with the three years we were apart."

"I thought…" I paused to clear my throat, trying to stay calm. "I thought you were putting that behind us."

"I thought so too. Then Jos showed up, and I realized that any number of women could show up out of the blue with a kid, saying you were a daddy."

"Fuck," I laughed, so relieved, I nearly fell on my ass. "Is that what you're so worried about, girl?" She glared at me, and I could only laugh again. I dropped to my knees between her legs, my hands sliding around her waist and locking at the small of her back. "I can tell you right now, that isn't going to happen, Rory. Other than that bitch Steph, I didn't fuck anyone else while you were gone."

"Don't lie to me," she cried, trying to push me back.

I leaned in, kissing the corner of her mouth. "I wouldn't lie to you. Not ever. I felt dirty after Steph. I fucking hated myself, baby. We weren't technically together, but I felt like I'd cheated on you, and it was hard to face myself in the mirror after that." She began to relax, her lips opening slightly to give me access to her mouth.

I kissed her slowly, taking my time, savoring the taste of her on my tongue. When I pulled back,

I pressed a kiss to the center of her forehead. "I love you. I fucked up once, but I couldn't do it again. Please believe me."

"I-I do." She melted into me, her head landing on my shoulder. "I'm sorry. I guess I'm going a little crazy. Ever since Jos came, I've been all over the place."

One of my hands cupped her stomach. "I think we know why now, huh?" She laughed softly, nodding against my arm. I sighed contently. "Does this mean you're going to marry me now?"

Her head snapped up so fast, it was a wonder she didn't have whiplash. "What did you say?"

My brows lifted at the surprise on her face. "Ah, come on, girl. Marriage was always on the table. I was just waiting on you to get used to me a little more."

"You still have to ask me, mister," she growled, crossing her arms over her breasts as she leaned back and glared at me.

"Asking means I don't know your answer. But I already do, so there's no reason to ask."

She slapped my chest. "Don't pull that alpha shit with me today, Matthew Reid. I will seriously kick your ass right now."

"Girl, you already have me on my knees, isn't that enough?" Her bottom lip pouted out, and I knew I couldn't tease her anymore. I clasped her left hand, lifted it to my lips, and kissed her ring finger. "Rory, I want to spend the rest of my life with you. I'll love and cherish you until the day I die. Please, baby, please marry me."

I expected her to give me that smile that lit me on fire from the inside out, but a sob escaped her instead. Her tears flooded down her cheeks, and she shook her head. My confidence in her answer nose-dived, and my heart stopped for the second time that day. I tightened my hold on her hand without realizing it. "Rory, please," I whispered in desperation.

"Yes!" she screamed, a laugh escaping her even as she sobbed again. "Of course, I'll marry you, dummy."

A relieved breath whooshed out of me, and I enfolded her in my arms, my heart finally kick-starting once again.

CHAPTER FIFTEEN

The ortho surgeon was able to fix both breaks in Tanner's arm with one surgery, which was great because then he wouldn't have to go through it again. I waited with the others until Tanner was put in ICU again once he was finished in the recovery unit. Everyone thought it would be best for him to spend at least one night in intensive care, just to be on the safe side considering everything his body had been through over the last month.

He was doing great, though, something I put down to the stubbornness of all the Reid men, my son included.

When I was finally allowed to see him, he was sound asleep, and I didn't want to bother him. Hawk and Gracie drove me back to the clubhouse so I could get some sleep somewhere other than in a hospital bed for once. The thought of sleeping snuggled up to my son for the first time in over a week sounded like bliss.

It was dinnertime when I got back, and Reid was sitting in his high chair beside his cousin. They were eating baked chicken chopped up with mac and cheese, peas, and mashed potatoes. The smell was so good, I moaned as soon as I walked into the kitchen.

"Fix yourself a plate," Aggie instructed me. "You look like you need some extra meat today, girly."

Piling my plate full, I sat down at the kitchen table where Willa, Raven, and Flick were already seated. I tore off a piece of my roll, scooping up a little of the mashed potatoes with it, and popped it into my mouth. As I chewed, Raven handed over a key to me.

"What's this?" I said, talking around the food in my mouth.

"The key to Tanner's room. We cleaned it up, changed the sheets, and scrubbed the bathroom. We figured that when Tanner is released from the hospital, he's not going to want you to be too far away, and really, I should have given you that room when you first got here. Sorry about that. Things have just been kind of crazy."

"You didn't have to do that," I rushed to assure her. "Reid and I are okay on the mat in the main room."

"Don't argue," Flick instructed. "The room wasn't being used anyway. Raven's right. We should have cleaned it out before now, but no one wanted to touch any of his stuff because…" She sighed heavily and shrugged. "It was hard when we thought he was gone, you know?"

I swallowed thickly, because I understood just how hard it had been, thinking I was never going to see Tanner again. I picked up my water glass, trying to get the food I'd just eaten dislodged from my throat because just the thought of Tanner dying was enough to make it close up.

"Thanks," I was finally able to choke out. I coughed to clear the last of my throat. "I should probably go back to Oakland soon and close out my apartment. Get us moved up here permanently. Plus, I can't let Grandpa's business go unattended for much longer. There are probably contracts that are already behind schedule."

"Good idea," Raven agreed. "I'll get some of the guys to follow you down in a few days with a moving truck. Essentials can be brought here, and the rest can go to Uncle Chaz's house… Or Tanner's?"

I lowered my gaze back to my dinner. "I'll let you know. I'm still figuring it out."

Tanner wanted me to give him a chance, but that didn't mean I was going to move in with him. Still, he would need someone to take care of him once he was out of the hospital. Matt lived with him, and I guess Rory did too now.

Hell, I didn't know what to do yet, so I just left it at that.

After dinner, I bathed Reid and got him ready for bed. As soon as he was asleep on the bed, I took a quick shower and then carefully slid in beside my son. Instantly, he cuddled into me, one chubby little fist balling in my shirt.

Smiling, I smoothed his dark curls back from his face and closed my eyes…

The buzzing of my phone pulled me from a peacefully dream-free sleep sometime later. Groaning, I reached out blindly, feeling for my cell phone to shut it up. My eyes squinted open to peek at the name on my screen, and I saw it was Matt. Sitting up in bed, I answered the call.

"Hello?"

"Hey." Tanner's voice filled my ear. "Did you sleep well?"

A glance at my phone's screen again showed me it was just after nine in the morning. I'd slept for over twelve hours. Shit. I started to panic, worried about Reid, but he was still sound asleep beside me. His butt was up in the air, his head turned away from me.

I fell back onto the pillows, my heart trying to return to a normal pace.

"Jos?" Tanner sounded anxious. "Baby, are you there?"

"Yeah, yeah. Sorry. I just realized I slept all night and Reid hadn't woken me up." Pushing a few strands of hair out of my face, I turned onto my side. "How are you feeling? Did you get any rest last night?"

"Woke up about five this morning, starving. Matt brought me some breakfast from Aggie's, though. Nothing like French toast and scrambled eggs with bacon to make a man feel alive again," he chuckled.

A smile lifted my lips. "I'm glad you're feeling well enough to eat. You always were a pig. Your lack of an appetite scared the hell out of me."

"I'm back in my private room. Can you come be with me?" His voice lowered. "I miss you."

My heart melted at his confession. "I miss you too," I admitted. "I'll come as soon as I get Reid ready for the day and find someone to babysit for me."

"Is he doing okay?" he asked. "I mean… Hell, I don't know what I mean. The only kids I've been around are Bash's, and even then, I don't have all that much interaction with them."

"He's doing fine. Actually, he and Max seem to be best friends at the moment. Which is a good thing because he hasn't been missing me too much while I've been busy this past week."

"When can I meet him?"

The uncertainty I heard underneath his usually cocky tone left me speechless for a moment. "Tanner, are you nervous to meet your son?"

"Hell yeah, I am. What if he doesn't like me? What if I fuck it up? What if I fuck him up?" He blew out a frustrated breath. "I'm not exactly in the best shape at the moment to show him any attention. What if he wants to play with me, and I can't?"

"He's not even two," I reminded him. "I think you can relax. He's not going to want to pass a ball with you anytime soon. Just relax. Reid will love you."

"Fuck, I hope so."

I bit into my bottom lip, melting a little more at the thought he cared so much about what his son would think of him that he was insecure. "I'll be there soon. Give me about an hour, okay?"

"Just you?"

"I really don't want to expose Reid to the germs of the hospital unless I absolutely have to. Plus, I think your first meeting with each other should be somewhere you're both comfortable," I explained.

"Yeah. You're probably right." He paused for a moment before speaking again. "Someone will drive you over. Don't go anywhere alone."

"I already promised you I wouldn't, Tanner," I reminded him. "Do you need anything? Clothes? Food?"

"Some fucking underwear would be nice," he grumbled. "But as long as you're here, I don't need anything else."

Damn it, when did he get all charming? It made my heart skip a beat. "I'll bring you some clothes," I promised. "Sit tight. I'll be there as soon as I can."

"Just be careful, baby."

I dressed and got Reid ready for the day. Flick was babysitting the younger kids today, so I left Reid with her so he could play with Max and Lexa. Breakfast sandwiches were waiting in the kitchen, and I snatched up one as I tossed the gym bag full of Tanner's clothes over my shoulder.

"You ready?" Colt asked as I walked out the back door.

"Guess you are my chauffeur for the day, huh?" I bit down on the biscuit loaded with scrambled eggs, sausage, and cheese with a thick slice of tomato.

"You guessed right," he said. "You ready?"

"Yeah, let's go."

It was easier to ride with Colt than Jet. Colt just seemed friendlier than his oldest brother. I relaxed into the passenger seat of his fiancée's car as he pulled into traffic. "How is Kelli today?"

"She's still sore, but doing okay. Quinn is taking care of her for me today because Kelli wants to do too much on her own. Damn stubborn woman," he groused as he drove through town.

"She seems nice," I commented casually.

He snorted. "Nice as in girl-next-door, or nice as in she will smile while she kicks you in the balls?"

I laughed. "The latter," I admitted. "But she has such a pretty smile."

He grinned. "She has many pretty body parts, actually," he assured me with a wink. "And now they're all mine."

"Good for you."

Spider was standing outside of Tanner's door today, and I gave him a warm smile as I approached, making sure to keep my eyes off the deadly spider inked on his neck. "Willa said to give you these," I told him as I passed him a paper bag full of breakfast sandwiches. "And you're not allowed to share with anyone, because she made them herself."

He narrowed his eyes on the bag. "She wasn't supposed to be out of bed."

"Relax. Staying in bed all day would drive anyone crazy. She needs to stretch her legs a little every now and then." I patted him on the shoulder and walked around him, pushing open the door.

Tanner was sitting up in bed. His casted arm was propped up on a stack of pillows, and his gaze was on the TV set hanging in the corner of the room until I walked in.

Hitting mute on his remote, he gave me an easy grin. "Hey, beautiful. You look like you got some rest."

"I did." Tossing the gym bag on the foot of his bed, I unzipped it and pulled out a change of clothes for him. Underwear, sweat pants, and a T-shirt would have to be more comfortable than the thin hospital gown he was currently in.

"How about a shower?" I suggested.

His eyebrows bobbed up and down. "Fuck yeah."

I slapped at his leg. "For you and only you."

"Spoilsport," he grumbled.

"I'll get Spider to help you get to the bathroom."

"I can walk to the damn bathroom on my own," he complained.

"When's the last time you walked anywhere?"

"This morning, when I had to piss."

"Oh, okay then." I walked into the bathroom and turned on the shower. The stall was narrow as hell, but I didn't plan on getting in there with him. Going back to the bed, I urged him up. "Let me find something to wrap the cast in so it doesn't get wet."

"There's a plastic bag in the top drawer over there. I saw it earlier when that nagging nurse wanted me to piss in some bottle." I crossed to the little dresser and bent, searching for it. When I straightened, bag in hand, it was to find his eyes glued to my ass. "What?" he asked innocently.

"Perv," I teased, wrapping the trash bag around his cast so that the entire thing was covered.

"You have a really great ass, baby," he informed me with a smug look on his handsome face.

Shaking my head at him, I got him to stand. He was a little shaky on his feet, so I supported him by putting his arm that wasn't in a cast over my shoulder, and I guided him into the bathroom. All he had on was the hospital gown, so I tossed that aside, making sure to keep my eyes above his waist while he got under the spray.

"Fuck, that feels good," he groaned, leaning into the jets.

There was a plastic pan full of toiletries that I made good use of. I had to get him to bend so I could wash his hair, then soaped him up with the tiny bottle of body wash. Even though he'd lost a lot of weight and muscle mass during his three weeks of captivity, he was still a huge man, so I had to use the body wash sparingly to make sure his entire body was clean.

When I touched his back, tears burned my eyes, and I sucked in a deep breath before I could stroke the red, tender flesh that had been flash-burned from the truck exploding. He shivered as I gently ran my soapy fingers over the large area. "Does that hurt?" I whispered.

"It itches a lot, but it doesn't hurt at all now." He glanced at me over his shoulder, his blue eyes darkening when he saw the tears glazing my eyes. "Don't cry, baby. It's just a scratch."

"Stop," I choked out. "Don't play it off as nothing. You could have died, Tanner."

"It'll take more than that to get rid of me." He leaned into my touch. "Can you scratch right there, sweetheart? It's itching like a bitch right now."

I scratched as tenderly as I could, and he sighed like he was in heaven. But I didn't want to chance damaging what was just starting to heal, so I finished his back and moved on to the rest of his body.

When I got to the bottom half of his body, I paused.

Having been enjoying my ministrations, he didn't like that I'd suddenly stopped. "Keep going," he commanded. "Your hands feel so good, Jos."

I could tell just how much he was liking what I was doing. His cock was at full attention, pointing straight at me. I sucked in a shuddery breath. "How can you be this hard when you're as weak as a newborn colt?"

Grinning, he shrugged. "It's your hands on me, Jos. I could be dead, and I'd still get this hard if you touched me."

My skin heated with pleasure. "Don't think you're going to get lucky, mister. You're in no condition for any of that."

He winked at me, the look in his magnetic blue eyes wicked. "Whatever you say, beautiful."

Sighing, I finished washing him, making sure to keep my touch impersonal as I washed everything. He groaned when I rubbed my soaped hands over his balls then along his cock. "So good," he grunted.

I jerked back, slapping him on the ass. "Stop that," I ordered. "I told you, you are in no condition for sex."

His head tilted to the side as his brows lifted. "What about a hand job?"

"Tanner Reid, you're nothing but trouble." Shaking my head at him, I turned off the water and grabbed a towel. The terry cloth was thin, so it took two of them to get him dry. I used a third to wrap around his waist for the walk back to the bed.

I helped him dress then eased him down on the bed. By the time the covers were pulled up over him, he was breathing hard. "Fuck, I need a nap after all that."

"Sleep. It will be good for you." I started straightening up his room, needing something to do other than sitting in the chair beside the bed and watching television for who knew how long.

"I'm hungry," he said with a yawn. "Is it lunchtime yet?"

"You still have a few hours before they serve it," I picked up my phone from where I'd left it earlier. "I can get someone to bring you something from Aggie's, though. All you have to do is tell me what you want, and she'll make it for you."

"Burger and fries. Some sweet iced tea to drink. Maybe some onion rings, too. Chocolate cake."

I blinked at him for a second before laughing and sending Raven a quick text. Ten seconds later, she told me she was having one of the brothers bring it over.

"Should be about forty-five minutes," I told him. "You going to be okay until then?"

"Depends." I lifted my brows at him. "You gonna come snuggle up with me and keep me company, or you gonna clean this place from top to bottom?"

I dropped the trash into the wastebasket and washed my hands. "Depends."

"On?"

"On whether you want to snuggle with me or not."

He scooted over on the bed, making room for me. Grinning, I climbed in beside him after kicking off my shoes. Seconds later, my head was on his chest, and his casted arm was draped over my waist.

"Yeah, I can wait for the food now," he muttered, closing his eyes. "Gonna take a nap, babe."

"Sleep," I urged. "I'll be here when you wake up."

CHAPTER SIXTEEN

TANNER

Bash and Matt sat on either side of my bed, their faces grim as they watched me closely. I shifted, trying to find a more comfortable position on the uncomfortable mattress. It was pretty useless, but it was worth a try.

"I'll take two," Bash finally said with a grunt.

I passed him two cards, waiting for my little brother to make up his mind. "Two," he muttered eventually.

I took one for myself and waited patiently for them to show me their cards.

"Two pair," Matt said, showing his double threes and queens.

Bash dropped his cards on the rolling table. "I got a flush. All diamonds."

I laughed, placing my four of a kind on the table between them. "Four sixes, bitches."

"I hate playing poker with you," Matt complained. "I don't know how, because I watch you like a hawk, but I know you cheat."

"I would never cheat you, little bro," I told him with a grin as I pulled in my jackpot.

"Sure," he grumbled. "I'm done."

"You always were a sore loser," Bash said with an amused twist of his lips.

"And you're not?" Matt countered. "If he weren't in a hospital bed, you know you'd be kicking his ass for cheating."

"Probably," my cousin admitted.

A knock on the door had all three of us looking up. Doc Robertson walked in dressed in his white coat and green scrub pants. He had his iPad in his hand and a cordial smile on his face as he entered the room.

When he saw me, he shook his head. "You've been here for four days, and I still don't know how you're able to even sit up considering the condition you were found in. I'm tempted to run tests to make sure you are human."

"How much longer you plan on keeping me in here, Doc?" I was itching to get out of this place. I felt better, and I'd even had a few physical therapy sessions to help me regain some of the strength in my legs again. I was tired of being cooped up in this small-ass room. I wanted to be home—or at the least, back at the clubhouse—so I could sleep in a decent bed.

Preferably with Jos.

"Your labs look good, and everything else is healing nicely," Doc commented. "But I would feel better if you stayed another few days."

"How many is your definition of a 'few,' Doc?"

"If you're still doing this well on Monday, I'll release you," he assured me.

Monday. Four more days. Fuck, I was going to start climbing the walls before then.

"Until then, I want to see you up walking throughout the day like you have been. Your muscles were starting to atrophy, which is what I'm the most concerned about at this point. But you're doing great considering…"

"Yeah," I muttered.

Considering I'd been tortured for three weeks, kept alive with an IV that pushed fluids into me, and given zero food. My body had been put through the kind of pain that would have easily broken a lesser man in minutes. Fontana was a sadistic bastard. He'd gotten off on making me scream, but he didn't get what he wanted. Even when he threatened Jos, I'd somehow kept my mouth shut.

I craved his blood.

I wanted to be his Angel of Death. Wanted to watch the life fade from his eyes when I put a bullet in his head.

"After you're released, I still want you to have regular physical therapy," Doc continued. "I think twice a week for a month should be good, and then once the cast comes off your arm, your surgeon will want you to have some PT on that as well."

"Whatever you say, Doc," I told him, pushing down my hate for Fontana to give the doctor a careless grin.

His expression turned more serious, and he opened the door to glance out before shutting it again and coming closer to the bed. Lowering his voice, he looked at Bash. "Bates has been asking me about Tanner having a skull fracture."

"What have you told him?"

Doc shrugged. "That I can't discuss my patient's condition with him. He asked me if it was possible Tanner has amnesia."

"And?"

"I told him it was possible. Why the hell is the sheriff asking me about this?"

Bash scrubbed a hand over his jaw. "Don't worry about it, Doc. He's just being nosy. If he keeps asking, just tell him Tanner has a skull fracture, and you're unsure when he is likely to regain his memory of the accident."

The doctor's gaze went from Bash to Matt and finally settled on me. "Bates has a vested interest in you not remembering?"

"Something like that," I answered.

"Right. Well, I hope you get him taken care of soon." He put his iPad in his large coat pocket. "Keep up the good work, Tanner. I'll stop by again tomorrow to check on your progress."

The three of us were silent until the door shut behind the man.

Alone again, Matt released a vicious curse. "We gotta take out Bates soon, man. We can't just sit back and let that motherfucker run loose. He's a danger to everyone."

"We have to play this smart, though," Bash reminded him. "I'm just as hungry for his blood as you are, but the bastard can't disappear right now. It would be too obvious we did it. Plus, he could lead us to Fontana. We have eyes on him, so for now, we have to bide our time."

"Fuck, I hate this shit." Matt stood, stabbing his fingers into his hair as he walked to the window, glaring out at the darkened sky. "I feel useless as hell right now."

"Save your energy for when we find Fontana," Bash said. "And don't let your guard down for a single second." His blue eyes landed on me. "You keeping that gun close, right?"

There was a gun in the hidden compartment of my rolling table. I put it under my pillow when I went to sleep every night. Knowing that it was close helped me sleep easier at night. "Don't worry about me. You just keep Jos and Reid safe."

"We sent five brothers with her, plus her dad, to get her things from Oakland," he assured me. "She's safe, cousin. Don't worry about her."

"I'm more worried about the threats closer to home than in Oakland." If Bates touched her, took her and my son to Fontana, I would crush his skull with my bare hands. "Bates is getting nervous if he's asking Doc about my condition. I'm a liability to him right now. One he would be all too happy to make disappear for a second time. But there are brothers guarding my door day and night. He knows he can't get to me in here. Jos is a different story, though. She's making noise about getting Uncle Chaz's business commitments taken care of and I've been able to hold her off, but that stubborn female isn't going to listen much longer."

"I'll watch over her myself," Bash promised.

"Me too," Matt vowed. "Stop worrying about her, brother. We've got your woman covered until you're able to do it yourself."

That made me relax a little, but I couldn't stop worrying about her and Reid. Whenever she wasn't with me, I was on edge.

"It's getting late. We should let you get some rest." Bash stood, gathering up all the cards and putting them back in the poker set we'd been playing with since dinner. "Spider is going to be guarding the door tonight. If you need anything, just yell out for him. I'll bring you breakfast in the morning."

"Thank fuck. Those eggs they try to make me eat here are nasty as hell. I don't know how people don't die from food poisoning when they're in the hospital." I leaned my head back into the pillows. They were my own from home, so they were comfortable, unlike the flat ones the hospital used. "Bring Jos with you tomorrow."

"Get some rest," Matt instructed, grabbing his things. "The faster you recover, the faster you can get out of here."

"Yeah, yeah. Stop nagging, Mom."

He punched me lightly in my good arm. "Don't make me kick your ass, bro. You know I can take you."

"You wish, bitch."

Chuckling, he followed Bash out the door. "Later."

As the door shut behind them, I caught a glimpse of Spider standing in the doorway. Trying to relax, I picked up the remote to the small TV mounted in the corner of the room. There was nothing on but kid shows and crappy sitcoms. Even the sports channels were boring as hell.

Muting the television, I grabbed my phone.

"Hello?"

The sound of her voice calmed all the noise in my head, and I closed my eyes. "How did the move go? Did you get all your stuff?"

"I didn't have much, just a few boxes of books, clothes, and all of Reid's stuff. With all the help, we got it loaded in less than two hours. Grandpa's house is a mess right now, though, until

I can get it all put away. But I'm too tired tonight to do it. It can wait for now."

My eyes snapped open again. "Why didn't you take it to my house?"

"Um, because I don't live there. Grandpa left me his house and the business to run. Reid and I will move in there once this lockdown bullshit is lifted."

"Jos," I growled. "I want you to live with me. You and our son are my responsibility now. I want to take care of you both. Please move in with me."

There was a long pause on her end, one that set my nerves on edge all over again. Finally, she let out a harsh huff. "If you really want to live with me, then you'll move in to Grandpa's house with us. There isn't enough room for your brother and his growing family plus us."

"Growing family...?"

"Oh please, don't tell me you didn't know Rory is pregnant. It's all everyone is whispering about here at the clubhouse right now."

"No, I didn't know. Matt hasn't said anything." I was going to beat his ass in the morning for keeping me in the dark about it. I was happy for him, thrilled to be an uncle. He should have told me.

"Well, don't stress over it. I'm not sure they've actually made any announcements, but it's kind of hard to hide the fact that she's been losing her breakfast a lot lately when everyone is confined to the same four walls for so long." I heard her moving around and pictured her sitting in the middle of the bed with her legs tucked up under her.

"What are you doing?" I asked quietly.

"Flipping through the channels in your room. There is nothing good on, but I'm too tired to socialize."

"What did you usually do in the evenings when you lived in Oakland?" The time she'd been living away from me made me curious about her life.

"I didn't watch television, if that's what you're asking. I was working two jobs just to pay the bills and for childcare, so things that weren't a necessity weren't important. Mostly, I read if I had the night off. Or just played with Reid."

"Sounds like you were pretty busy." I didn't like that she'd taken on so much all by herself, but I wasn't going to lecture or yell at her for not telling me about our son. I'd fucked up spectacularly when I did what I did, but at the time, I thought I was protecting her. "Do you need anything, Jos? What can I do to help take the strain off you with taking care of Reid?"

I heard her swallow loudly before she spoke. "The fact that you're alive and getting better every day is all I need from you right now, Tanner. We can talk about other things later, once you're back to normal."

"You really going to let me move in with you?"

"We can talk about that later too," she said after another pause. "You might not be ready for that yet."

"I might not, or you might not?" Because I sure as fuck knew I was ready. I wanted to be with my family, and that was Jos and our kid.

"No comment," she muttered.

"I don't want to push you, baby. But fuck, it's so hard to be away from you even for a few hours,"

191

I told her honestly, needing her to know how it was for me. "The last two years, I was going crazy missing you."

"Tanner…"

"Don't say anything. I just wanted you to know. I fucked up, Jos. I seriously thought you were better off without me."

"How?" she demanded, suddenly pissed. "How could you possibly think I would be better off without you? I was in love with you."

Goddamn it, I didn't like that she was saying "was." I ached for her to still love me.

"When you got to Creswell Springs that last time, your mom called Uncle Chaz. He was in his office, and I overheard her bitching at him," I said. "She said you were turning down a summer internship in LA to come visit with your dad and grandpa. She said the MC was fucking up your life all over again, and that everyone was being selfish. There was a lot more bitching, and then she said if we cared about you, we would let you have a life away from the trouble that follows the MC around."

"I can see my mom doing that," she muttered. "But you should know that it was all bullshit. There wasn't an internship. I wasn't even talking about college or anything at that point. I wanted to stay here and help out Grandpa. Not just because I wanted to be closer to you—although that was a huge part of it—but because I love it here. I've never really felt like I belonged anywhere but here. My mom couldn't care less about me being around, Tanner. She just doesn't want my dad to get my attention."

The sadness in her voice destroyed me. "I'm sorry, sweetheart. If I'd known, I wouldn't have pulled that shit."

"You crushed me that morning," she whispered, her voice catching. "The night before was amazing, and I thought you really wanted me."

"I did. I fucking do!" I half shouted in my need for her to believe me. "Jos, baby, you're everything I've ever wanted. That first night with you was hard to get over, but that last night was so goddamn perfect, it ruined me."

"Tanner…" My name came out breathy, making my body respond as if she'd physically touched me.

And then the phone went completely silent.

CHAPTER SEVENTEEN

As soon as Raider stopped the car in front of the hospital, I was running.

Nothing short of death could have kept me away after what Tanner said earlier. I asked Raven to watch Reid for the night then stopped the first brother I came to in the parking lot and begged him to take me to the hospital.

I ran through the lobby and punched the elevator call button repeatedly until it finally opened for me. Pressing the right floor, I shifted impatiently from one foot to the other until the doors slid open, and then I was running again.

Spider saw me coming, his eyes wide at the sight I must have been. "Everything okay?" he asked, concern on his handsome face.

I stopped in front of him. "I decided to spend the night here. Don't let the nurses bother us."

A sly grin lifted his lips. "Will do." With a wink, he pushed open the door. "Yo, T. You got company, man."

"Who is it…" His voice trailed off when he saw me, and he sat up straighter. "Jos. Fuck, you just hung up on me and wouldn't answer when I called back. I thought you were pissed at me."

"Nope." I stepped into the room and waited until Spider closed it again before pulling off my jacket. And my T-shirt.

Tanner's throat bobbed when he swallowed as he watched me. With each step that brought me closer to his bed, I took off another piece of clothing. My bra fell to the floor, followed by my pajama pants and then my panties.

"Holy fuck," he groaned. "You're so damn beautiful, baby."

I climbed up on the narrow bed, straddling his lap, but before I could kiss him, he was already cupping the back of my head, pulling me in closer. His lips were hungry, ravishing my mouth. His casted hand skimmed down my back until his fingers squeezed my ass, pressing me down into the hardness of his cock.

"Shit," he growled. "God, you taste so good."

I kissed a path from his lips down his throat to his chest. I felt possessed, unable to stop until we were both satisfied. My hands trailed lower, cupping him through his sweats and stroking twice before diving under the material and pulling him free. I licked my way down his hard stomach until I reached his cock.

"Jos," he grunted, his fingers tangling in my hair as I swallowed half of him.

I sucked and licked until he was drenched then got back on my knees and positioned myself right over him. Wrapping my fingers around the base, I guided him into me slowly. The tip had barely entered me before he was cursing, his head thrown back in ecstasy.

"You feel so good, baby," he groaned. Catching the back of my head again, he forced my mouth to crash down on his. He thrust his tongue into my mouth, teasing, playing with me as I sat down fully on his cock, taking all of him inside me.

I felt stretched almost to the point of pain, but it felt so damn good. Tanner kissed me, distracting me until my body was able to adjust to his size invading my body. When the slight pain eased, I began to move my hips, riding him slowly. Feeling his groan vibrate in his chest, I pulled back, worried that maybe he wasn't ready for this yet.

Before I could ask if he was okay, he leaned forward, pressing his forehead to mine as he helped me move my hips faster, riding him harder. His breath came in harsh pants, his fingers biting into my flesh.

"Fuck, I'm about to come, sweetheart," he gritted out. "Can I come in you? Is it safe?"

Oh hell! I'd forgotten about protection. How could I possibly take that risk when he hadn't even met the kid he already had?

"I'm still not on the pill," I moaned.

"Shit," he muttered, lifting me off him just as thick, white streams released from his tip. I cupped my hands around his shaft, stroking him through his orgasm.

Breathing hard, he released me to use his shirt to clean up the mess, then pulled me back down onto his cock. He was still rock hard even after coming so forcefully, but I wasn't going to complain. Not when I was still aching for him. "Sorry, baby. That had been building for a while. I'll last longer this time, I promise."

I fell against his chest, my hips already rocking as I rode him once again. "You sure you're okay? Nothing hurts? You don't feel weak?"

"Weak is the last thing I feel right now, sweetheart. And the only thing that hurts is my cock because I want to come inside your tight little pussy." He nipped at my shoulder, his fingers biting into my hips once more. "Fuck me all night, Jos. Give me what I've been dying for the past two years."

My walls clenched around his thickness, and I gave him exactly what he wanted.

***

A pitiful moan jerked me awake.

For a moment, I thought it was Reid having a bad dream, but when I opened my eyes, it was Tanner who was making that heartbreaking sound. His head moved restlessly on the pillow, his heart pounding under my ear.

I lifted my head to see sweat beading on his brow.

"Tanner?" I murmured softly, trying not to startle him.

"Fuck you," he growled. "Shut your filthy mouth about her... Jos... Stay away from Jos!"

My stomach bottomed out because he wasn't just pissed, he sounded a little scared too. Swallowing my own fear, I tapped him lightly on the face. "Tanner, baby. Wake up. It's just a dream. It's okay. Wake up."

His eyes snapped open, and he sucked in a few gasps before focusing on me. "Jos?" I gave him a weak smile, and he wrapped his arms around me so tight it was hard to breathe for a moment.

"Thank God you're here. Baby, ah fuck. I can't let him get to you."

I kissed his chest, my free hand stroking up his side in an attempt to soothe him. "He won't." I tried to reassure him. "You're here now. You won't let him touch me."

He shuddered so hard, it made my own body shake. "I'll gut him if he even looks at you," he vowed, his arms tightening so forcefully it was painful. I mewled at the discomfort, and he instantly eased his hold. "Sorry. I'm sorry." He kissed my forehead over and over again. "I'm so sorry, sweetheart."

"It's okay. Just relax," I urged. "Try to go back to sleep."

He lay back down, and I moved so more of my body was on top of his. I'd put on one of his extra T-shirts earlier after going to the bathroom, and it hiked up as I wrapped one leg over both of his. His four-fingered hand was under me, rubbing over my hips in a nonsexual way, but he still caused goose bumps to pop up. It felt so good to have him touch me, and soon I was falling back to sleep.

Heavy footsteps entering the room had my eyes popping open sometime later. I lifted my eyes to see who Spider had let enter and saw Bash holding two takeout bags from Aggie's and a drink carrier full of coffee. The smells coming from both were making my stomach growl, and I sat up beside Tanner, who was still sound asleep.

Feeling me move disturbed him, though, and he jerked awake, his hands grabbing me when I tried to shift off the bed. "Don't leave me," he grumbled, half asleep. "Need you here."

"Yo, cousin," Bash said as he dropped everything on the rolling chair. "Brought you some breakfast."

Tanner woke fully, his stomach growling even louder than my own. I untangled myself, blushing when Bash's brows lifted at the sight of me in only an oversized T-shirt. Considering Tanner was completely naked under the covers, there was no way we could deny what we'd been doing the night before.

"Good to see you've got your strength back," Bash said dryly.

"Fuck off," Tanner grumbled. "Jos, put some clothes on, damn it."

"That was my plan," I assured him, picking up my stack of clothes from where I'd dropped them and walking into the bathroom. Quickly, I pulled on all my clothes and folded his shirt as I crossed back to the bed.

Tanner and Bash were already tearing into their breakfast sandwiches like wild wolves who hadn't eaten in days. I was a little worried for my fingers as I snatched the paper bag and pulled out my biscuit. Sometimes I wondered if the Reid men were human or beasts.

"What's on the agenda for the day?" Tanner asked after stuffing the last of his breakfast into his mouth and reaching for his coffee.

"You have more physical therapy today," I reminded him, taking a sip of my own coffee after loading it with plenty of cream and sugar. "And I need to go to the office and start taking care of business. Barker Construction isn't going to last long if I don't start working."

"Damn, can't it wait until I'm out of here so I can go with you?"

I shook my head, popping the last of my biscuit into his mouth. "Nope. It's already piling up too much to wait even another day."

"Bash, go with her," he ordered.

"I can't. I've got to go into the garage. Flick is dealing with all the office stuff for Uncle Jack's business, but Trigger and I have to figure out something to do about everything else. Gracie is turning it over to her dad, and Trigger wants me to step in as a partner." He tossed the trash into the wastebasket, stretching his large body.

"Well, someone better go with her. I don't want her going anywhere alone."

"I hear you, man. Don't worry. Your female will be protected." Bash nodded toward the door. "I'll take her back to the clubhouse now. Her dad will go with her, and I'll get one of the other brothers to help out. Okay?"

"Yeah," he said, but he didn't look happy about any of it. "And Reid? Who's going to be taking care of him?"

"You don't have to worry about the boy. Raven and the other women are spoiling him rotten. He's happy, Tanner. Doesn't have a care in the world. Right, Jos?"

I nodded, smiling reassuringly. "I'm a little jealous, actually. He doesn't even miss me anymore."

"Fuck, I just want to get out of here and see him," Tanner muttered. "This waiting sucks balls."

"A few more days won't kill you," his cousin assured him. "Just focus on getting back on your feet, and we'll make sure your woman and son are taken care of."

A knock on the door was followed by Spider pushing it open to let in a nurse. She was pushing her meds cart. "Good morning, Mr. Reid. Time for your medication and vitals before I turn everything over to the day shift nurse."

I watched as she took his blood pressure and temperature before giving him a cup of his normal morning meds. Now that his IV was out, everything was in pill form, but I'd made them tell me what everything was the first time he'd taken them. I eyeballed each one as he took it, making sure he didn't get anything he shouldn't, or didn't miss any he should.

Once she was gone and Tanner was comfortable again, I reluctantly asked Bash to take me back. I didn't want to leave, but I really did have to take care of work. It wasn't just about me not upholding my grandpa's legacy. He had men who relied on their jobs, jobs that wouldn't be there if I didn't start taking care of the company.

Leaning over the bed rail, I brushed a kiss over Tanner's lips. "I'll come back for dinner, okay?"

"You going to spend the night again?" he asked with a smirk, his four-fingered hand grabbing my ass and squeezing.

"That we will have to wait and see about, mister." I kissed him again before forcing myself to step back. "Be good today. Don't give anyone any trouble."

"I can't make that promise, sweetheart."

"Try, and I'll consider staying again tonight," I offered.

"Fuck. I'll do my best." I was at the door before he called out to me again. "Jos." I glanced back at him, curious as to that odd note in his voice. "Give Reid a hug for me, okay?"

My heart melted at the uncertainty on his face. Smiling, I nodded. "I will, babe."

CHAPTER EIGHTEEN

As quietly as I could, I opened the bedroom door and stuck my head out enough so I could look down the hall. Glancing left then right, I breathed a sigh of relief that there wasn't anyone going to their room or lingering to talk.

Still being as quiet as I could, I shut the door behind me and was about to make a run for the back door when the door across from mine opened and Colt leaned against the doorframe, crossing his massive arms over his chest.

I swallowed my groan and glared at him. "Why are you hiding like that?"

"Why are you sneaking out?" he countered.

"Because I'm getting cabin fever. You can't keep me locked in this room forever, Colt Hannigan."

"Did Doc say you could do regular activities?" His brows rose when I mumbled a reply. "I'm sorry, I didn't hear that. Was that yes or no?"

"No!" I yelled, feeling like a petulant child being scolded. "But he also didn't tell me to stay holed up in bed all damn day either. I'm fine, Colt. There's no pain." Much, I thought. But hell would freeze over before I admitted that. "And I'm not tired. I just want to go outside and breathe in the fresh air."

Pushing away from the doorframe, he took my hands in both of his. "I just don't want you to overdo it," he said in a quiet, gentle voice. "You're just getting over being shot, baby. I don't want you to have a setback."

"But I'm fine now," I assured him, melting into him. It felt good to have someone to lean on. Other than the rare occasions when my mom wasn't stuck up my father's ass, I hadn't ever had anyone who cared about my well-being. Now, it seemed I had an entire family, with Colt front and center. Always worrying about how I was feeling, if I needed anything. Loving me.

"All right, let's go outside for a little while. But then promise me you'll take it easy the rest of the day."

I might have actually jumped up and down in excitement if I'd known he wouldn't send me straight back to bed. I curbed the urge and linked my fingers through his as we walked through the clubhouse.

"Hey, Kelli," one of the ol' ladies called when she saw me. "How are you feeling, honey?"

"I'm good."

"Good to see you up, Kelli," another said with a warm smile as we passed through the main room.

I returned her smile, but I kept walking, needing to see the outside world, breathe in the fresh air. Our bedroom was starting to smell stale to me, the four walls seeming to close in on me a little more every hour I was stuck in there.

Instead of going out the front, Colt led me through the kitchen, grabbing a paper plate and loading a few sandwiches onto it from one of the platters that always seemed to be set up this time of day. Handing me two waters, he took my hand again and walked out to one of the picnic tables outside.

The back parking lot was like a ghost town. No cars, no motorcycles, and no people scattered around eating or just shooting the shit. The air wasn't as chilly as it had been lately, but Colt still sat close to me, as if trying to keep me warm with his nearness. Picking up one of the sandwiches, he offered it to me.

"Eat, then we'll walk around the parking lot a little before you go back to bed."

I didn't argue, figuring I would only be wasting my breath if I tried to just yet. Instead, I bit into the turkey and cheese sandwich. I didn't know if it was the fresh air or if I was just that hungry, but I devoured the meat and bread like I hadn't eaten in days rather than just a few hours.

Quinn had brought me a tray of oatmeal and toast that morning for breakfast, but she had been too busy helping to watch all the kids running around the clubhouse to have time to keep me company. Flick had come to take the tray a while later once I was finished, but she had been busy too. I knew everyone had responsibilities while we were on lockdown, and I would rather have been helping them out than stuck in that damn room all by myself.

"How is Tanner?" I asked before washing down my last bite with my water.

"Good. Should be coming home in a few days." He finished off one sandwich and picked up another. "I've been meaning to tell you..." He glanced around to double-check no one was nearby, but he still lowered his head to whisper at my ear. "If you see Bates, you need to avoid him as much as possible. Don't trust anything he tells you or answer any questions he might ask."

I widened my eyes at the seriousness of his face. "Okay. Not that I would talk to that creep anyway, but why?"

"He's responsible for what happened to Tanner."

Holy shit. I wasn't expecting that. "And he's still alive?" I asked incredulously.

"For now." Colt kissed my lips tenderly before lifting his head. "I mean it, Kelli. Turn and walk in the other direction if you see that motherfucker coming. And if you can't get rid of him, call me. Actually, call me, regardless. I want to know if that bastard is anywhere near you."

"Yeah, okay. Avoidance is key. Gotcha." I yawned, but when I saw the way his eyes darkened, I quickly snapped my mouth shut. "No, no, no. I'm fine. I'm allowed to yawn without you freaking out."

"You're tiring yourself out, baby. Please go back to our room and take a nap," he urged, his face full of so much concern, my heart turned to goo.

But I wasn't about to let his sinful good looks and that loving glaze in his eyes ruin my time outside. The air was crisp, and the sun was shining down on us. I was soaking up the Vitamin D and enjoying the slight breeze that was lifting my hair every few minutes. "I'm sick and tired of napping.

I'm fine. Have a little trust in me to know my own limitations."

"You're so fucking stubborn," he grumbled, glaring at me as he took another bite of his sandwich.

Grinning, I kissed his jaw as he chewed. "You love me, though."

"So fucking much." Dropping the sandwich on the plate, he turned so one leg was on either side of the bench and pulled me between his thighs. I snuggled against him, pillowing my head on his chest. "I just want to take care of you. Make sure you're okay. I want to spend the rest of my life with you, and I don't want to risk missing even one day of that. I nearly lost you, Kelli. I can't go through that shit again."

I sighed, a mixture of exasperation and annoyance. "Okay, fine. I'll go back to bed… After you tell me everything that's been going on lately that I've missed."

He didn't tell me much unless I made him, and I knew it was because he didn't want to "stress me out." But not knowing what was going on around me was stressing me out more than actually knowing, damn it.

Blowing out a frustrated exhale, he picked up his sandwich again. "Everyone seems to be pregnant lately, including Rory. You know about Bates. The election is only a few days away, so we need to make sure Jenks has all the support he can get. Willa said she's having triplets, so everyone is watching her like she's going to explode any minute, and she's getting grumpy over it. And Quinn and Raider are getting married like next week or some crazy shit."

I blinked at his rundown of everything I'd apparently missed. I knew from what little I'd been able to catch that Gracie and Willa were both pregnant, but I'd missed the news that Rory was and that Willa was carrying multiples. Holy shit, that was scary. Quinn hadn't told me she was getting married so soon, and I wanted to be upset she hadn't mentioned it, but I understood how busy she'd been the last few days.

"How did I miss all of that? You've been holding out on me."

"I've been kind of busy, sweetheart. I've barely had time to sleep lately." He kissed the top of my head.

"Yeah, I noticed. I've missed you."

He tightened his arm around me. "I'm sorry, baby. Things will slow down soon. Then we can start making wedding plans."

"Ugh. You're not going to want a big wedding, are you?"

"Just the family," he assured me, but that didn't make me feel any better. By family, I knew he meant the entire MC family. If that included everyone, it wouldn't be nearly as small as I would have liked.

"How about this. Me and you fly to the Bahamas, get married on the beach, come back, and have a reception afterward. Like two, maybe three weeks afterward," I suggested.

He watched me for a long moment, and I just sat there, waiting for him to shoot me down.

"Is that what you really want?" he finally asked.

My heart jumped that he wasn't outright telling me no. "Yeah, it kind of is. I don't want a big wedding. Hell, I don't want much of a wedding, period. I never thought I would even get married, but here I am with a ring on my finger and a sexy biker asking me to make plans with him." I shrugged, feeling out of sorts. "I love you and I want to marry you, but… I don't know. I just want this to be about me and you."

"Okay," he said, surprising me with how easily he was giving me what I wanted. "As soon as everything is calm here, we'll take a trip to the Bahamas or wherever you want. I'll marry you on the beach. Fuck, I'll marry you anywhere you can think of. I just want you."

"And that's why I love you," I said with a choked laugh, happier than I could ever remember being in my entire life. "Now I have something to plan while I'm being held prisoner in our room. This should be fun, though."

Standing, he tossed the paper plate in the huge trash can by the door then came back and offered me his hand. "Come on. You promised," he half whined, half growled when I just looked at his palm. "Please go back to bed and rest."

Sighing heavily, I took his hand and stood. "Only because you said please."

CHAPTER NINETEEN

I finished stacking all the contracts that needed my immediate attention and picked them up. This was going to take more than a few hours in the office to sort out, so I would have to take the most pressing things home with me.

Grabbing my phone and my keys, I walked out of the small work trailer and headed for my car. Dad's motorcycle was parked right beside it, but he must have gone out to one of the work sites with one of the foremen to check on that shipment I'd been concerned about earlier.

I wasn't worried, though. I wasn't expecting anything to happen to little ol' me. There was no reason they would even bother with me. Still, I knew it would make Tanner feel better, so I hadn't complained. One or two of the MC brothers had come out to help Dad watch out for me, but they'd changed so regularly throughout the day, I'd stopped paying attention.

"All done?"

I lifted my head from the top paper I'd been glancing over, frustrated because we were going to have to get—beg for, actually—an extension on the contract for the repairs to the grocery store that were supposed to be finished in the next week. It was past dinnertime, the sun long gone, so all I had to see by were the security lights that hung off the ends of the work trailer. Hawk stood on the other side of my car, leaning his arms on the roof. His blond hair was covered with a black beanie. The thick coat he wore hid his cut, but I knew it was under there. The Angel's Halo VP didn't go anywhere without that leather vest on.

I'd had a mad crush on him and his brothers when I was growing up, but those feelings all disappeared when Tanner caught my full attention. Still, Hawk Hannigan was fun to look at.

"I didn't see you there," I told him, shifting the stack of files to my other arm as I unlocked my car with a push of the key fob. "Have you been here all day?"

"Butch called to say he was going out to one of the sites, and then Brady had to go to work. I figured I had you covered."

I opened the back door and dropped my load beside Reid's car seat before straightening. "I wasn't questioning your ability to watch my back," I assured him with an easy smile. "I just figured you would be watching over Gracie."

His lips pressed into a grim line. "I would be, but she says I'm too much of a distraction. Jet and Colt take turns sitting around out front or drinking coffee with the receptionist. She's probably already home now, though."

I glanced around for his motorcycle, frowning when I didn't see one. "You've been standing out here in the cold the whole time? You could have come in and warmed up."

"It's too noisy when the heating turns on," he explained. "I can't hear if someone is pulling up from in there. Gotta be vigilant with Bates walking around."

I tossed him the keys over the top of the car. "Since you don't have a ride, you drive while I deal with a few phone calls."

Grinning, he walked around the car and folded his huge frame behind the wheel. I was already on the phone with a client before I shut the passenger door.

"Put your seat belt on," Hawk grumbled as he pulled out onto the highway.

Rolling my eyes at him, I did, continuing my conversation with the thankfully sympathetic man on the other end of the phone. Grandpa's passing had reached everyone's ears, so I didn't have to offer too many incentives to get the extension, which would keep us from coming out in the negative in the process.

Ending the call, I dropped my phone in my lap with a relieved exhale.

"You're pretty good at that for a newbie. Uncle Chaz taught you well."

My heart squeezed, thinking of my grandpa, but I warmed at the compliment that the man I'd adored my entire life had prepared me well to be his successor. "Thanks. I loved every summer I spent following him around, playing his secretary. It was fun, so I didn't consider it work, but now I see he was subtly grooming me to fill his shoes one day."

"Just imagine, one day all of that will belong to Reid." His brow knitted together. "Just like my kid will inherit a part of the bar."

"Scary, isn't it?" I asked with a small smile. "That our kids will be in charge of all this in the future."

"I just don't want to fuck them up before they can," he admitted, his tone somber.

"With you and Gracie as parents?" I shook my head. "Your kid will be one of the lucky ones, Hawk."

He took his gaze off the road to glance at me, a ghost of a smile teasing at his lips. "It's good to have you home, Jos."

I started to laugh, but it turned into a scream of fright when my car was bumped from behind.

We swerved, crossing into oncoming traffic. Hawk cursed violently, but he somehow avoided the eighteen-wheeler going the other direction. He got control just as we hit a deep ditch on the other side of the road and came to a jarring stop.

I was shaking, my heart beating me to death with how hard it was pounding against my ribs. Beside me, Hawk was already on his phone, but I was glad he hadn't gotten out yet even though two passing vehicles had already stopped up above us. Their hazard lights were on, and I saw the shadows of the drivers running toward us.

"Jos, are you okay?" he demanded as he waited for the person on the other end of the phone to answer. "Jos? Hey, honey, talk to me."

Somehow, I was able to swallow my fear and finally nod. "I'm okay. Just…just really shaken up."

"Nothing hurts?"

"No," I said weakly.

He hit the overhead light, his eyes scanning over me. Then I heard the murmur of a deep voice from the phone. "Hawk?"

"Bash, fuck, someone rammed Jos's car and knocked us off the road. They must have had their lights off when they came up behind us, because I didn't see anyone tailing us before it happened."

There was a knock on my window since it was closer to the road, and I squeaked in fright. With the glare of the overhead light, it was hard to see out, but I caught the outline of a thin man, and I cracked my window just enough to hear what he was saying.

"Hey, you guys okay in there? Anyone need medical attention?"

"Fine," I assured him, but my voice came out weak. I cleared my throat, trying to make it stronger. "Just shaken up."

"I called the cops. Man, that truck with the lights off scared the hell out of me. Didn't see the driver, but I bet it was drunken teenagers doing one of those damn challenges they're always causing trouble with."

I wasn't sure that was who'd hit us at all. It struck me then that someone had just tried to kill Hawk and me, and I already knew who was at the top of the list of suspects. And this guy, who only wanted to help, had just called him to report the accident.

***

Bash and Jet showed up before the cops did. Not Bates, but one of his deputies. By then, Hawk and I had already gotten out to assess the damage.

The back end of my little car was smashed in, but it could have been so much worse if Hawk hadn't acted fast and kept us from becoming a crushed tin can.

I shuddered, remembering the brightness of that eighteen-wheeler's headlights, the sound of his horn screaming through the air as we narrowly missed impact with each other. The truck wouldn't have even noticed the jar from it, but it would have hit me dead center. Right at that moment, Reid could have been motherless.

I owed Hawk my life.

"Easy there." Jet's voice was soft as he caught me around the waist when I began to sway. "Just take deep breaths. You're okay."

I turned my head, pressing my face into his coat as the tears spilled out of me. I'd almost died. I was nearly taken away from my son. Hawk could have died without ever having seen his own child being born.

"You sure she doesn't need medical attention?" the deputy asked, sincerely concerned for me.

"She's just in shock," I heard Hawk excuse. "It was a close call."

"Well, I have statements from all the witnesses and the two of you," the young man said, closing his notebook. "We'll get a wrecker out here to haul the car into the station, see if we can get any paint off the bumper to analyze. We will also be looking around for any signs of trucks with damage. Might be able to find the person who did this if we're lucky."

I wasn't going to hold my breath.

With the release of my tears, it was as if I also unleashed my anger. I turned, ready to start cussing out the deputy, tell him exactly who I thought—who I fucking knew—did this. Jet must have sensed my rage, because he pulled my head back to his chest, locking me into place while he quickly made an excuse to get me home.

I was put in the back of Raven's SUV. Jet climbed in behind me, putting my seat belt on me like I was a child. Moments later, Bash and Hawk joined us, Hawk carrying all the files I'd forgotten in the back seat of my car.

"Wait," I said when Bash started the vehicle. "Reid's car seat."

"It's not usable now, Jos," he explained. "Anytime you're in an accident, you have to replace the car seat. Don't worry. We have a few extra ones at the clubhouse."

My phone went off, but it took me a few seconds to realize it before I picked it up. "Hello?"

"Hey, baby. You coming tonight?" Tanner's voice was full of mischief, and I suddenly had to fight a new wave of tears. "I was good all day."

"H-Hey," I murmured, leaning my head against the window and closing my eyes. "I… I, um, I don't think I'll be able to make it in tonight."

"What's wrong?" he demanded, sounding alert.

"There…" I swallowed hard, scrubbing a hand over my damp cheeks. "There was kind of an accident a little while ago—"

"Are you okay?" he asked before I could finish. "Is Reid?"

"We're both fine." I gave him a quick replay of what happened on the way back to the clubhouse after work. By the time I was done, I could feel his tension crackling through the phone.

"Don't leave the clubhouse," he growled and hung up.

I sat there a little hurt he hadn't said more, but before I could think about it further, Bash was pulling through the compound gate. Hawk got out, opening my door and helping me to the ground. My legs felt shaky, my stomach tossing. I clenched my hands into fists because they were still shaking and walked into the clubhouse.

Raven and Flick were there as soon as I stepped through the door. "Come on," Raven ordered, guiding me toward the bedrooms. "Let's get you sorted."

I didn't question her, just followed her while Flick followed behind. We went to Tanner's room, and Flick helped me take a shower. When I came out, drying my hair with a towel, it was to find Raven sitting on the bed with three red plastic cups and a bottle of Jameson.

"Where's Reid?" I asked, my voice still devoid of strength. "I should get him ready for bed. It's already past—"

"Stop worrying about Reid. He's already asleep in my room with Max," Raven assured me. "Just relax. How are you feeling? Do you have whiplash?"

"My muscles ache because they are so tense, but otherwise, I'm fine." I took a sip from the cup and welcomed the burn from the whiskey, but it did nothing to alleviate the chill that seemed to be freezing my blood. Alcohol probably wasn't the best idea when my stomach was tossing, but I welcomed the numbness it would hopefully bring.

There was a tap on the door, and Raven walked over to open it. Kelli stepped in, and Raven shut the door behind her before crossing to the bed. "Sit down so I can tell my brother you were resting."

"I've been sitting all day," the beautiful brunette grumbled, but she sat at the end of the bed. "I'm tired of sitting." Her eyes fell on me. "How you feeling, Jos?"

I could only shrug as I lifted the cup to my lips again and took another sip.

Flick sat down beside me, sandwiching me between her and Raven. "Looks like Bates is getting nervous," she murmured so quietly I had to strain to hear her.

Raven nodded. "We need to deal with him sooner rather than later. I get Bash doesn't want to draw attention to the club, but Bates has too much to lose if he thinks Tanner might narc on him."

"They have eyes on Bates, so was it really him who did this?" They were talking over my head as if I weren't even there, but I was okay with that. I didn't think I could participate given how I was feeling right then, so I just sat there drinking my Jameson and listening. Kelli leaned forward, listening intently, taking the offered cup of whiskey Raven handed out.

"Maybe he snuck out without our eyes seeing. Or maybe he has a lackey doing his dirty work," Raven suggested. "But I don't see him having a partner. He seems like too much of a greedy, distrustful sonofabitch, so I can't see him confiding in someone or giving them the responsibility to take out Jos to prove a point."

"I have an idea." Kelli's voice was just as quiet as the other two, but there was something on her face that screamed at me to pay attention.

"We're listening," Raven assured her.

"That stuff you gave Colt to drug me with—"

"I said I'm sorry about that, didn't I?" Raven groused as my eyes widened. What the hell had happened that Colt would drug Kelli? I thought they were crazy in love. "When will you drop that? Fuck."

Kelli rolled her eyes. "Shut up and listen for a second, blondie."

Flick snickered. "I love how alike you two are."

"You want to hear my idea or not?"

"Please enlighten us," Raven said dryly.

"How much of it do you think it would take to kill him?"

"Shit," I whispered, downing the last of my whiskey and then holding the cup out for Raven to refill.

"He's a big guy, but he's got to be over fifty by now," Flick stated. "And I've seen what he orders when he has meals at Aggie's. His heart is a ticking time bomb. Shouldn't take too much, I wouldn't think."

"We would need to make it look like he's got a problem," Raven commented, deep in thought. "It would eat up my supply of the little cocktail I make for the boys, but it would be worth it."

"Are we bringing the guys in on this?" Flick asked, which seemed to be the most worrisome question among the three of them.

"Fewer people who know, the better," Kelli said with a lift of her shoulders, then her eyes were on me. "You gonna narc on us?"

I thought back to how hurt Tanner had been when I first saw him. The way my heart stopped both times he coded. How terrified I was when I saw those oncoming lights headed straight for me. Tipping my cup back, I swallowed the contents in one gulp. "No," I said, wiping my mouth with the back of my hand. "I'm in."

CHAPTER TWENTY

The sound of the door softly clicking shut had my eyes snapping open. The buzz I'd had from the Jameson was all but gone now, replaced by a fear that suddenly had me sweating. I didn't move, didn't even breathe as I waited, listening.

Seconds later, a curse filled the air as the person who'd just entered the bedroom collided with Reid's pack 'n play. Relief washed over me, and I sat up, snapping on the light.

"Tanner?" I blinked at the man standing at the end of the bed. He was dressed in sweats and a T-shirt, his hair standing on end like he'd been running his fingers through it repeatedly. His beard was still disorderly, but I kind of liked it on him.

"You were expecting someone else to climb in bed with you?" he demanded, brows lifted, a snarl already starting to form on his usually smug face.

"What are you doing here?" I countered, my concern for him overriding the irritation at the jealousy beginning to flood from him. "Doc said you weren't going to be released until Monday at the earliest."

"Doc can go fuck himself. I'm not lying around in some damn bed while the woman I love is being run down. You're mine, Jos. It's my job to keep you safe, and all I was doing was lying there doing nothing." He jerked his T-shirt over his head as he crossed the remaining distance to the bed.

I was still caught up on the whole "woman I love" thing and didn't have the brain power to realize what he was doing until his hands pushed me gently back onto the pillows, his lips already attacking my neck.

He loved me?

A groan that sounded pained left him as he cupped my breast in his four-fingered hand. "Baby." He shuddered. "Fuck, I'm never letting you out of my sight again."

"Tanner." I arched up into his touch, my body melting for him. "Oh God, that feels so good."

The old T-shirt and pajama shorts I was wearing disappeared in no time, and then he was pushing deep inside of me. "Jesus," he groaned. "Every time I slide into this pussy, I feel like I'm home."

I couldn't speak, could barely breathe as he thrust in and out of me, driving me crazy with his lips on my body, staking his claim.

My release snuck up on me, and I cried out his name before I could stop myself. He grinned down at me. "That's right, baby. Scream my name. Let this whole goddamn place know who is fucking you."

My nails bit into his hips as the agony of pleasure made me convulse. His grin disappeared, replaced by a look of tormented ecstasy. He went stiff over me, and then I felt his cock grow harder, thicker inside me. His release filled me up, but I couldn't find the will to care.

Woman I love.

Those words floated through my mind as he fell on top of me, his weight a comfort. Kissing my lips softly, he buried his face in my neck. "I was so damn scared," he confessed in a raspy whisper. "You said there was an accident, and a nightmare of shit flashed through my head."

I stroked my hands down his sides, mindful of the tender flesh on his back. "Tanner…"

"Mm?" He sounded sleepy, but his lips were sucking lazily on my neck while his cock started to wake up all over again deep inside me.

"Did you mean it?" I whispered, half afraid to even ask.

"That I was scared? Yeah, Jos. I was terrified."

"N-No…" I pushed on his shoulder, urging him back so I could see his face. "The part…when you said 'the woman I love.' Did you mean it?"

The confusion on his face cleared, to be replaced by an expression I'd never seen on him before. Vulnerability. "Yeah," he said after a minute had passed. "I love you, Jos. I always have."

Tears surprised us both by falling over my lashes. "Y-you really mean that?"

He touched his lips to my tears, kissing them away. "Never meant anything more in my life, sweetheart."

"I love you too," I whispered.

His entire body jerked. Lifting his head, he met my gaze, a look of wonder in those magnetic blues. "Jos. Fuck. Beautiful, fuck." He grew even harder inside me, and I arched up into him, desperate for him all over again.

**

My mom clock went off at six, as usual. I slowly shifted out from under Tanner's hold. His casted arm was locked around my waist, but he was deep asleep. It took a moment, but I was finally able to free myself.

I took a quick shower then tossed on the first things I could find, a pair of jeans and a black hoodie that was older than my son. Pulling my curls into a ponytail, I left Tanner still sleeping.

Down the hall, Raven's door was open, but I still knocked, not wanting to walk in without warning in case Bash was naked or something. But it was only Raven in there when I entered. There was a crib against one wall and a cot across from it, the bed right in the middle of the room.

Reid and Max were already awake, both of them standing up in the crib, talking happily in their baby language. In the cot, Lexa was slowly waking up but not happy about it. "Mommy, my arm hurts," she whined.

"I know, baby," Raven said with a sigh. "We'll go to the doctor and see what's going on, my love."

"Is her wound not healing right?" I asked, concerned.

"No, it's healing fine. It's just giving her more pain the last few days. I think she might have some torn tendons or something. She might need an MRI." She sighed heavily. "That's going to be fun."

"Do you want me to watch Max for you?" I offered, picking up Reid. He already had a fresh diaper and, by the looks of it, so did Max.

"Thanks, but I'm taking him with me. Flick and I have some grocery shopping to do, and Max needs some fresh air. Jet and Raider are going to go with us." She picked up her phone. "Do you need anything? I'll add it to my list."

"I'm good." I kissed Reid's cheek, and he wrapped his arms around my neck. That was his favorite spot. It seemed that was his father's favorite spot too. "Tanner checked himself out of the hospital last night. Should I be worried he's not recovered enough?"

"Bash told me," she said with a grimace. "I wouldn't be too concerned. He's basically recovered except for some muscle issues. That was why Doc wanted to keep him in the hospital a few more days, to make sure he gets enough physical therapy. It's easier to have him home, though. We'll make it work, Jos. Don't worry."

"Milk," Reid complained. "Milk, Momma."

"Okay, okay." I rearranged him on my hip. "Be careful going into town."

"Tell Tanner you're going with me later. Flick and Kelli are making plans with their men too."

"Will do," I called as I left the room and headed for the kitchen.

In the main room, others were just starting to wake up, but the kitchen was in full swing when I walked in. There was a sippy cup already waiting for Reid in the fridge with his name on it, filled with milk. Beside it sat a small cup of grapes and cut-up strawberries.

"Thank you, whoever did this," I said to the room at large.

"We figured you would be busy this morning," Quinn said with a smile. "We're just glad Tanner is home."

"Me too," I admitted.

"Here, girl." Aggie pushed a plate into my hands. It had three sandwiches on it, thick slices of toast with fried eggs and crispy bacon. My stomach growled just looking at them. "Go feed yourself and your man. It's about time the Reid boys met each other, don't you think?"

CHAPTER TWENTY ONE

TANNER

The overhead light turning on had me reaching for the pillow to cover my face. "Go away, Matt," I groaned.

"Sorry, no Matt here." Jos's sweet voice reached me, sounding amused. "We brought breakfast, Daddy."

My entire body went still, even my heart stopped beating. Daddy. Lifting my head, I saw Jos walking toward our bed, a kid in her arms who looked so much like Max, I had to blink a few times before I realized it wasn't. He had a sippy cup full of milk in one hand, some kind of kiddie cup I'd seen the other little ones have snacks in held in the other.

I started to sit up quickly, only to remember I was naked under the blankets.

"Easy," Jos said with a soft laugh. "He's got all the same parts you do, so you don't have to freak out he's going to see your dick."

Cursing under my breath, I finished sitting up in bed, putting my back against the headboard and keeping the blanket tucked at my waist. All my moving around had caught Reid's attention. His blue eyes, a Reid trademark if ever there was one, were glued to me. Curiosity was plain on his face as he watched me from the safety of his mother's arms.

Jos stopped beside the bed, placing a plate I'd just noticed on the nightstand before sitting beside me. Reid moved to sit on the bed and pulled out a grape. He offered it to his mother. Her smile was so kind, so full of love, and I'd never seen her look more beautiful.

"No thank you, baby boy. Ask Daddy if he wants a bite."

Reid frowned then pointed at me. Jos nodded, her smile encouraging. "Yes, Reid. That's your daddy."

I held my breath, waiting to see what he would do, while a million things went through my mind. Would he like me? Accept me? Fuck, he wasn't even two, but this little boy's opinion of me was suddenly the only thing that mattered.

The hand holding the grape lifted in my direction fearlessly. "Bite?"

I leaned forward, letting him feed it to me, making a growling noise as I sucked the piece of fruit into my mouth. He squealed in delight, giggling, and it was my new favorite sound. A small chunk of strawberry was produced from the snack cup next, which he promptly fed to me. I growled again, eating it up, my beard tickling his chubby little hand.

While he giggled and screamed with delight, I drank in the sight of my son in the flesh. Fuck, he was a beautiful boy. Dark, curly hair. Bright blue eyes that were full of the kind of happiness every kid should have. There was no denying he was a

Reid. Anyone would know what clan he belonged to from a mile away.

And he was mine.

I'd helped create him.

This beautiful little boy was half me, half his mother, and the best thing I'd ever made in my life.

A lump filled my throat, and all I wanted in the world right then was to hug him. Not wanting to scare him, I held out both my hands to him, letting him decide for himself. His attention was immediately pulled to my cast. "Boo-boo?"

"Yes, honey. Daddy has a boo-boo," Jos murmured softly, but I could still hear the catch in her voice.

His chin puckered, and he crawled forward until he could reach me. Pushing up to his knees, he carefully patted my cast. It was still painful from surgery, and even his light pat was enough to send pain-filled vibrations all the way up my arm, but I didn't even flinch, too caught up in the moment of having my son touch me so fearlessly. "Boo-boo," he said with the kind of empathy only the innocent possessed.

When he kissed my cast, the magical medicine I'd seen Raven and Bash use countless times on Lexa and Max, a lump filled my throat. Reid lifted his head, his eyes wide as if to ask "All better?"

"Thanks, buddy," I choked out, more overcome with emotions than I could ever remember being in my entire life. "That feels much better now."

He beamed then climbed into my lap. "Milk, Momma," he said, holding out his hands toward his sippy cup.

Jos handed over the sippy and the snack cups then leaned back against the headboard beside me before placing the plate she'd brought with her between us. "Aggie made breakfast. I don't know about you, but I'm starving."

She picked up one of the three sandwiches, biting into it like she hadn't eaten in days.

With my good arm holding Reid loosely against me, I wasn't even going to try using my casted one to pick up the sandwich. My stomach came a poor second to holding my son for the first time. I leaned back, enjoying this first meeting, praying like mad I didn't ever fuck it up. I loved this kid like crazy already. He was mine to raise into a man, to protect with my life.

I won't let him down.

Fuck, I'd missed almost two years of this because of my own stupidity. I never should have let Jos go, should have just been my usual selfish self and kept her as close as possible and damn the consequences. Then I wouldn't have missed out on watching her stomach grow with our baby, or holding him when he was first pushed into the world, or loving him and his mother with every breath that left my body.

"Bite?" Reid offered me another grape, but before I could move to take it and make him giggle, Jos was offering him a bite of her sandwich. He bit into it hungrily, protesting with a squeal when she went to pull away. The snack cup was tossed into my lap as he crawled over to his mother for more.

She tore off a piece of the sandwich and offered it to him.

"The look on your face is sweet and heartbreaking all at the same time," she murmured softly. "He's a Reid, Tanner. He's going to follow the food every time."

"He's mine, Jos. He's going to follow *you*. Every time," I told her, leaning in for a quick kiss. "I can't blame him. You're just so damn beautiful, it's hard to resist."

Pink filled her cheeks, and she pushed the plate into my now-free hand. "Eat. Then you need to walk around a little so your muscles don't get too stiff. Doc said the more walking you do, the better. But I still want you to take things easy. No heavy lifting, and when Reid naps, I would like for you to as well."

"Napping with my son sounds like fun," I said with a shrug. "But only if you're napping with us too."

That got me a roll of her eyes. "I have work to do. Actually, I'm glad I brought so much with me last night. Now I won't have to go to the office."

I paused, my sandwich inches away from my mouth, my stomach clenching in dread. "You aren't going anywhere without me from now on, we clear?" I couldn't risk her life. I fucking *wouldn't* risk it. She was too important to me. I loved this woman, and I wasn't going to let anyone try to take her away from me.

Her teeth bit into her bottom lip for a second before she sighed. "I can't stay locked up in the clubhouse, Tanner. I have work to do. Men who are relying on me to run Barker Construction so they will have a job, health care, a paycheck to pay their bills and feed their families."

"And you can work. I'm just going to be with you." I finally took a bite of my breakfast, mentally groaning at the taste of perfectly salted eggs and crispy bacon. Food had never tasted so good, but maybe that was because I'd taken it for granted all my life. Three weeks without a single crumb to eat made a man appreciate the food placed in front of him.

"I don't want to argue with you about this," she muttered grumpily. Standing, she dusted a few crumbs off her shirt then the bed where Reid was just finishing up the last bite of his portion of the sandwich.

As soon as it was stuffed into his mouth, he eyeballed my sandwich, and I gladly tore off a piece like his mother had done and offered it to him. He moved so he was leaning against me before accepting the offered food.

"I'm going to get us some coffee," Jos announced. "You two carry on cuddling."

"Can I have another sandwich?" I asked with a pout.

"Pretty sure Aggie would make you a hundred sandwiches."

"One more is plenty." I took another bite, chewing slowly.

"Coffee and another breakfast sandwich coming up," she said with a smile. "You two be good."

Reid didn't even pay attention when she left the room. He was too interested in looking at my four-fingered hand. I glanced down at where my pinkie should have been, remembering the excruciating pain when Fontana had sliced it off with a cigar cutter. It hadn't been quick. The whole thing took minutes while I'd tried to hold in my screams of agony, not wanting to give the evil bastard the satisfaction of hearing how much pain I was truly in.

When it was over, he'd lit a cigar and used it to stanch the bleeding, searing the wound closed.

It was mostly healed now, as were my fingernail beds, but the memories would stay with me for the rest of my life.

"How about some TV, little dude?" I offered, grabbing the remote off the nightstand to distract us both from my missing finger.

I turned it on to some Disney cartoon thing about two puppies. Reid shifted, getting more comfortable, and laid his head on my side.

By the time Jos returned, I was just as engrossed in the damn show as my son was and even had a favorite of the two puppies.

"You two look like you've been doing this forever," Jos commented as she took my empty plate and replaced it with one that held another sandwich and some pancakes. "Lexa wanted pancakes, so Raven made you a few too."

Reid was already tearing apart the top pancake, sprinkling powdered sugar all over the bed. Jos didn't seem to care, though. The sheets were going to need washing anyway after our crazy night, so I didn't give a shit either. Let the kid play. He was having fun, and I was enjoying watching him.

The crazy thing was, I saw so much of myself in him. Not just in looks, but in personality. We hadn't even met until that morning, but he acted so much like me, it made me grin.

When we were finished eating, the show was over, and Reid didn't seem as interested in the next show. He climbed off the end of the bed and toddled over to the corner of the room where his toys were.

"He's going to be busy for the next fifteen minutes or so," Jos informed me, following my gaze. "You should take a shower. Everyone was asking how you are, and they want to see with their own eyes that you're okay."

I let my eyes trace over her, a new hunger starting to gnaw at my gut. "I guess you can't join me, huh?"

A matching hunger began to burn in her gaze, but she shook her head reluctantly. "Sorry, babe. Reid will destroy this place if someone doesn't watch him."

"Damn," I grumbled, but I leaned in for a kiss. "Later?"

"Definitely," she promised, a dazed look on her beautiful face.

***

As soon as I walked into the main room of the clubhouse, it turned into pure mayhem. Ol' ladies and sheep alike surrounded me, hugging me, patting me on the back, sobbing that they were so happy I was okay.

I let the majority of them hug me, but I made sure to keep it short, not wanting to give Jos a reason to feel jealous or insecure.

Eventually, though, I just had to tell them to give me some room to breathe, because they were all smothering me.

As soon as they went back to doing what they should have been doing, Reid toddled up to me with a toothy grin on his face, a book in his hands. "Da-Da, up!"

Heart contracting, I bent and lifted him up, looking down at the book in his hands. "Whatcha got, little dude?"

"Play?" he asked hopefully.

"Soon, son. Daddy's got some work to do." I kissed the top of his head, hugging him tight.

"Yo, T!" Spider called out as he came through the door. "Let's go to church, man."

"Right behind you," I told him and reluctantly put Reid on his feet. "Go play, buddy. We will play later."

He toddled back over to the group of kids playing, and I started up the steps to Bash's office.

The room was already crowded with my fellow brothers, and I shut the door behind me as I stepped inside. There wasn't an empty seat, but I was tired of sitting around, so when someone offered me their chair, I shook my head. "I'm good."

Bash slapped his hand on the desk, calling church to order. "Let's get this shit started. We got a lot to cover and not a lot of time to do it in."

"Last night, someone tried to kill me and Jos," Hawk announced, but only a few of the brothers seemed to find this news, most of them probably having already known about it. "Jos was most likely the target, and we all know why."

"Why can't we just put a bullet in Bates and be done with it?" Butch demanded, his face red with anger. "That sonofabitch is responsible for Tanner being handed over to fucking Fontana. And now he tries to kill my daughter? My grandson could be an orphan right now if the sheriff had his way. The bastard needs to meet the Angel of Death."

I grunted an agreement.

"Brother, I would be happy to end that motherfucker, but we have to be smart about this," Hawk told him. "With Tanner coming back from the dead, we suddenly have all eyes on us. The election is Tuesday. If we wait until then, the attention will be on Jenks and Campbell."

"Bates isn't the only issue at hand," Bash announced. "Fontana is still out there somewhere. I want all eyes open for anything even remotely suspicious. That fucker could be anywhere, biding his time to take one or all of us out."

"We got other problems right now too," Matt said, bringing all eyes to him. "Who the fuck put something in the goddamn water and now all the females are getting pregnant?"

The room erupted in laughter, and I suddenly wondered what the women had been drinking. Because whatever it was, maybe I wanted to give Jos some of it too.

CHAPTER TWENTY TWO

With Max on my hip, I walked with Lexa into the exam room. She was still whining, and every time I saw her tears, the desire to eviscerate Fontana came back all over again. I hoped I'd killed whoever had shot my baby girl.

Maybe he had been one of the two I'd taken out that night.

But in my mind, Fontana was the cause of Lexa's tears. He was why she was in so much pain. Without him, she wouldn't have to go through any of this.

I held out my hand to her, and she trustingly placed the one that wasn't connected to her aching arm in it to steady herself as she climbed onto the exam table. I sat her brother down beside her, then tossed the diaper bag in one of the chairs against the opposite wall.

"Poor little lamb," Mable, Doc Robertson's oldest and sweetest nurse, said soothingly as she took Lexa's temperature and placed a blood pressure cuff on her good arm.

I rubbed Lexa's back while the cuff squeezed her arm, and she whined again. Max didn't like that his sister was so unhappy and tried to climb on top of her. Flick was just next door in the pharmacy getting me a few supplies for later and had offered to take him with her, but for some reason, I felt uneasy letting either of my babies out of my sight today. Call it mother's intuition, or paranoia after what happened to Jos and Hawk the night before, but I couldn't shake this feeling of unease.

I knew my best friend and soon-to-be sister-in-law would have protected my son with her life, but it freaked me out just thinking of not having him with me.

Fuck, I needed to calm down. My nerves were getting the better of me, and if I wasn't careful, I was going to have a full-on meltdown.

Mable finally finished up just as a knock came at the door, and Doc walked in. He smiled warmly at Lexa and produced two suckers as he approached the table. Max snatched his before I could even say a word, expertly ripping off the paper and stuffing it into his mouth, while Lexa was more hesitant.

Good girl.

Her allergies scared us all half to death, but now that she was getting older and questioning everyone who offered her food, I was able to relax a little more about her eating while I wasn't around. Still, I kept a supply of EpiPens everywhere.

Doc's smile increased. "No worries here, Lexa. I make sure that all the treats I get are made in a nut-free environment just for you."

Her smile was pitiful as she finally accepted the sucker and carefully unwrapped it before putting it in her mouth.

Doc's attention went straight to me. "Still hurting?"

I nodded. "It seems to be getting worse each day. I've been giving her anti-inflammatory pain relievers, but they don't even seem to put a dent in her pain."

"Lexa, honey, can I see your arm?" He crouched down so he was at an even level with her arm. She pulled up her sleeve, and I had to grit my teeth at the sight of the angry red scar from where the stitches had closed up the through and through. He shifted her arm, making her whimper, and I had to remind myself Doc was only trying to examine her, so I shouldn't punch him in the back of the head.

"Does it hurt more here…" He lightly touched the front of the wound, then the back. "…or here, sweetheart?"

"There," she sobbed when he pressed a little more firmly on the underside of her arm. "It hurts so bad, Mommy!"

I pulled her close to my chest, kissing the top of her head. "I know, baby. I'm so sorry."

After a few more seconds of feeling around, Doc straightened. "You know what I'm going to have to do, Raven."

I nodded, my gut twisting. Lexa was going to need an MRI to check to see if there was any damage caused by the bullet. She was going to have to be placed in some tiny-ass machine, and lie still for however long it took to get the pictures needed. That was a nightmare of epic proportions. I didn't want to have to put her through it, but we had to have answers as to why she was in so much pain.

"How soon can we get it done?" I asked.

"I'll get the order, and you can take it straight over to the hospital. I don't want to wait in case we need to go in there and repair something. This might be nothing but some growing pains and tender muscles, but it could also be something more."

"Yeah, okay," I said, outwardly calm. On the inside, I was praying this was just growing pains. Lexa had already been through so much. I didn't want her to have to go through surgery on top of everything else.

Ten minutes later, I exited the doctor's office. Jet and Flick were sitting in the waiting room and stood as soon as we came out. Max squirmed, wanting Flick, and I gladly handed him over. "Can you take him back to the clubhouse?" I asked her. "Lexa needs to go over to the hospital for the MRI."

"What's an MRI?" my daughter asked, her brow puckered in confusion and worry.

"A machine that's going to take pictures of your arm, baby," I explained patiently. "So we can see what's wrong and why you're in so much pain."

"Will it hurt?"

"No. It's just going to take a while to get all the pictures we need. Do you think you can lie on the little table really still for me?"

She nodded, but the anxiety didn't leave her face.

"Raider's outside," Flick said, taking the diaper bag from me. "I'll have him take me and this little monster home. Jet can go with you to the hospital."

My own anxiety skyrocketed at the idea of Max leaving my side, but I nodded. I guess I had to have Flick take him back, after all. He didn't need to be exposed to the germs of the hospital if he didn't need to. Hell, I didn't want to expose Lexa, but there was no getting around it.

Jet held his arms out to Lexa, and she let him pick her up, laying her head on his shoulder as we all walked outside together. Raider was waiting beside Quinn's car, but it didn't have a car seat yet, so Jet gave him the keys to my SUV while I grabbed Lexa's booster from the back seat.

Ten minutes later, we were in the radiology waiting room. It wasn't busy considering it was a Saturday, but that also meant less staff. Jet sat down with Lexa on his lap, her head once again cradled on his shoulder, while he rubbed her back.

I stood there watching them as I waited for the receptionist to appear so I could hand over the MRI order. Jet was so good with kids. I wanted him and Flick to be able to have babies of their own, but even if they couldn't, I knew he would be okay. They could adopt, and he would love them just the same.

As soon as the tech appeared, she took the order and waved us back. "You can't be in there with her during the procedure," the woman said. "But you can go in and help her get comfortable before the MRI starts. It will help calm her to know you're with her at first."

Lexa had to put on a hospital gown, which she didn't like, but the tech gave her a teddy bear to hold on to with her good arm while I helped her lie down on the narrow table and wrapped her in a blanket.

"I'm scared," Lexa whispered when she saw where she was going to be during the test.

I bent over her, kissing her brow. "Let's pretend you're in a cave with your teddy," I suggested. "Close your eyes and imagine you're on an adventure, but hold really, really still, okay? The less you move, the quicker it will be over."

The tech pushed the button to move the table back into the machine, and at first, Lexa whimpered in fright, but she quickly calmed down when I reminded her to close her eyes. Reluctantly, I followed the tech out when she directed me to.

"It shouldn't be too long," the woman said with a kind smile. "I'll bring her out as soon as we're done."

"Can't I wait here?"

She shook her head. "Kids tend to perform better when their parents aren't around. Just relax. I'll take good care of your little one."

My feeling of unease returned, but I walked through the door, back into the waiting room with Jet. For the first ten minutes, I tried to sit still, but it was agony. For the next ten, I paced the length of the waiting room, glancing at the door every thirty seconds. When another ten minutes passed, I was starting to feel sick.

"It's taking too long," I told my brother. "They should be done by now."

"Maybe she was moving around a lot. Just give it a little longer."

Ten, then fifteen minutes passed, and as each of those minutes ticked my, my stomach filled with dread.

"I can't take this anymore," I snapped and pushed open the door that led back to the MRI room.

The sound of Jet's booted feet echoed behind me, and I didn't understand why they were so loud. The machine was in a soundproof room, and the only way to speak to the person inside the MRI was through a microphone from the control room. But it still felt alien to me that there was zero sound coming from back there.

Then I rounded the corner and fought back a scream. Not because the tech was slumped over the control panel where she'd been sitting, a bullet between her lifeless eyes.

But because Lexa was gone.

The teddy bear was lying on the floor, and Lexa's clothes weren't where I'd folded them after helping her into the hospital gown.

"Motherfuck!" Jet roared as my knees gave out and I began to fall.

CHAPTER TWENTY THREE

One minute I was sitting with Trigger in Gracie's office, the next, my entire world seemed to be crashing down.

I still held the phone to my ear, could hear Raven's sobs in the background, each of them full of tortured rage that made my heart rate spike. Jet repeated himself again. "Lexa was taken during her MRI. The tech is dead. We have to figure this out. Now."

I still wasn't able to process it. My wife, the love of my life, sounded like she was being flayed alive.

My baby girl was gone.

Gracie snatched the phone out of my hand. "Hey, what's going on? Bash looks like he's turned into a statue." I met her gaze, silently begging her to tell me I heard it wrong. But as the seconds ticked by and she listened to the man on the other end, her face turned stony, and I knew it wasn't a mistake.

The woman was the sweetest person I'd ever met. If she looked like she was about to murder someone, then I knew it was real.

Finally snapping out of it, I jumped to my feet and grabbed my phone back. "Pull the camera footage from security. Get everyone moving. We have to find her."

"Security is here now. The place is going on lockdown, but I think the bastard is long gone by now. The cops will be here any minute, brother. Bates—"

"Bates is goddamn dead," I roared.

"I didn't hear that," Gracie said from behind me. "Nope. I'm pretending I didn't hear that so I can defend you later if I have to." She pushed on my back, and I turned to glare at her. "If I have to," she repeated, lowering her voice. "Don't make me have to, okay? Hide that fucking body really, really good."

"Raven!" Jet's yell pulled me back to the man on the other end of my phone. "Where the fuck are you going?"

I strained to listen, heard my brother-in-law curse and then his heavy breathing, as if he were running.

"Jet?"

"Bash, man, Raven just took off. She's already at the car!"

My stomach bottomed out. That damn woman. I had a million things to worry about right then, and she was taking off.

But I already knew where she was going.

Bates.

"Trigger, let's go," I called over my shoulder, but the retired army vet was already behind me. "Get your rifles," I told him once we were on the street. It was better to be prepared for anything and everything than not. "We might need a sniper."

My motorcycle was parked right out front of the law office, the street fairly deserted since it was Saturday morning. Trigger threw his leg over his own, going back to his house, while I headed for the first place I could think to look for Bates. His house.

Bates lived outside of town but within the county lines. It was a good twenty-minute drive to his place, but I was there in half that. Still, Raven had beaten me there, and I found her climbing through one of the windows, not seeming to care that his neighbors could see her if any of them so much as looked out their window.

A crash from inside had me barreling up the driveway from my motorcycle, and I quickly kicked open the front door just as I found Raven with a gun pointed in Bates's face. "Where is he?" she seethed, a mother bear desperate for her cub.

"Wh-What are you talking about?" he stuttered, eyeballing first the gun aimed right at his nose, then me.

"Answer her!" I roared. "Where the fuck is Fontana?"

"Wh-Who?"

Raven grabbed his shirt, pulling him in closer and pressing the gun flush against his forehead. She was slender, and the sheriff outweighed her by a good hundred and twenty pounds, but she was so enraged, she seemed to be even stronger than me all of a sudden. "Enzo Fontana took my baby. I know you work for him, you sick sonofabitch. You have five seconds to tell me where he is, or your brains are going to be all over your motherfucking couch!"

"I-I don't know anything about—"

"Raven!" I yelled when her finger started to squeeze the trigger, and I eased toward her. "He does know. Don't fucking kill him yet." When I could reach her, I wrapped an arm around her waist, not pulling her away, but letting her know I was there with her. We would figure this out.

We would find our daughter.

Her hand stayed steady, but I felt the rest of her body tremble. "She's probably so scared," Raven whispered. "And this bastard knows where she is. He has to."

"I-If you kill me, you'll never see her again," Bates warned. "They'll give you the needle for killing a cop."

She leaned in closer. "I don't see a cop around here. Just a spineless little pussy who is about to piss his pants. Tell me where Fontana is."

"I really don't know!" he screamed, sounding terrified, his bulldog-like face deathly pale.

"But you know something. You're his little bitch, right? You took him Tanner. You have to be able to contact him. Give me his number."

When he just kept his mouth shut, she lifted her knee, hitting him direct center in the balls. He wheezed out a whimper and fell to his knees. Grabbing him by the hair, she tilted his head up. Tears leaked from his eyes, his face almost purple from the pain. The gun moved from his temple to just under his chin. "Do you know what my husband will do to you?" He gulped, and she grinned so fucking evilly that it brought goose bumps to my skin. "That is nothing compared to what I will do to you, you motherfucker. I will skin you a-fucking-live."

"My phone," he gasped out. "The contact number is all I have, I swear. I didn't know he would take the kid. I wouldn't have let him do that."

"Sure, you wouldn't." She took the phone he offered up with shaking hands and tossed it to me.

I pulled up all his contacts, but it wasn't like he had it so obviously listed under Enzo Fontana. "What's the name?" I bit out, flipping down the list.

"Erick Frank," he said with a curse.

I found the name and hit connect. Two seconds later, a heavy laugh filled my ear. "Meet me at the spot, Bates. This is going to be fun." Then he hung up.

"Where's the spot?" I demanded.

"What spot?"

"Stop wasting my time!" I roared. "Fontana just thought I was you. He expects you to be at 'the spot.' Tell me where the fuck that is, or Raven is going to blow your brains out."

"Okay, okay," he cried when she pressed the metal up under his chin harder. "It's some ancient house out in the boonies. A good hour and a half from here. I've met him there a few times."

"Let's go," I ordered, grabbing him by the collar of his shirt and lifting him to his feet. "I don't have time to play games with you."

I marched him out to Quinn's car and tossed him in the back seat. Raven handed over the gun, and I got in beside the sheriff while she climbed behind the wheel. "Where am I going?"

"South."

CHAPTER TWENTY FOUR

TANNER

The sound of my kid's giggles was the most heart-soothing thing I'd ever heard. That I was the cause of them only made it that much better.

I was in my room, resting so Jos wouldn't worry, but I wasn't sleepy, so I was taking advantage of the moment to get to know my son better. He was a good kid, not a whiner, and I'd seen him sharing his toys earlier with the other kids. I also learned that he didn't like having Max taken away when they were playing, but Raven needed to take Lexa to the doctor, and for some reason, she wouldn't let the boy out of her sight.

A hard knock on my bedroom door irritated me because I didn't want to be interrupted while I was having a good time with Reid. But the person on the other side was impatient and opened the door without me inviting him in.

Colt walked in, my little brother right behind him. Two seconds later, Rory followed them in and bent down to scoop up Reid. "I'm just going to take him into our room, Tanner," she said with a grim smile. "Don't worry about him, okay?"

Before I could say anything, she was out the door again, shutting it behind her.

"What's going on?" I demanded, my gaze still on the closed door, already missing my son.

"Fontana took Lexa," Colt bit out. "Hospital security cameras showed the bastard sneaking into the radiology department through a back door and taking her. He killed the tech and took Lexa while Raven and Jet were in the waiting room right outside."

I was already on my feet before he'd shut his mouth. "Let's go."

"Raven ambushed Bates, and now she and Bash are taking him to some meetup with Fontana," Colt continued.

"Why do you keep trying to sell this?" I asked, both brows lifted. "I said, let's go."

"Rory still had Raven's keys," Matt said as we took the back exit. "I'll drive."

Colt climbed in the back, giving me the front passenger seat while my little brother got behind the wheel of the Charger. The powerful engine purred to life, and then Matt was burning rubber as he hit the gas and sped through the gates and out onto the road.

"Jet and Trigger are on their way south," Colt announced. "Bash texted Jet the address, and Trigger picked him up. Raider and Hawk are on their way too."

"Tell me you already packed the trunk," I gritted out.

Matt snorted. "Raven keeps all her vehicles loaded, brother. You should have seen the arsenal she pulled out when Fontana ambushed the memorial service for you and Warden."

"Momma bear was pissed, huh?" I muttered.

"You think she was mad then… She has to be about a million times worse now," Colt said with ice in his tone. "Rave will blow up the world to protect her kids, man."

I was beginning to understand that feeling.

My phone ringing pulled me from my inner musings. Seeing Jos's name on the screen, I muttered a curse but lifted it to my ear. "Baby, something came up. Rory has Reid."

"I was just in the fucking main room working!" she exploded, but even though she sounded upset, just hearing her voice calmed something in me. "You didn't think to tell me where you were going? Or even that you left, period?"

"Lexa was taken," I told her. "I had to go."

She was quiet for a long moment before blowing out a harsh breath. "You better be careful, do you hear me, Tanner Reid?"

"Yeah, sweetheart. I hear you."

A shuddering sigh left her. "I love you, dummy. Be safe, okay?"

"Love you, Jos. I'll be back before you even miss me," I promised.

"Too late," she muttered. "I mean it. Be careful." She hung up before I could comment.

It took over an hour to meet up with Bash and Raven. No sooner had Matt turned off the Charger than Trigger pulled up behind him in his truck, Jet in the passenger seat. Hawk and Raider followed suit moments later on their motorcycles.

I glanced around, not seeing buildings or so much as a shack. This place was off the beaten path, but it didn't look like there were any signs of life other than us.

Bash jerked Bates out of the back seat of Quinn's car by his shirt collar then slammed him up against the side of the car. "You better not be fucking with me, Bates, you little bitch. Anything happens to my daughter, and I'll make you eat your own cock."

"The house is a mile up the road over there," he rushed to assure the vibrating beast who had his hands at his throat. "I told you this place was in the boonies. The road is overgrown, but it's there, regardless."

"What's the layout of the place?" Trigger, who rarely spoke unless spoken to, demanded, already pulling one of his rifles from its case. "One-story house? Two? How many windows? Where is he most likely to be?"

Bates stuttered out the answers while Jet sketched out a crude draft of the details and Hawk and Colt unloaded the artillery from the trunk of Raven's Charger. I caught the Glock they tossed my way, then the three magazines that followed.

"That's all I can offer you in order for the rest of us to have some too," Colt said with a grimace. "Make every bullet count."

"Only need one," I growled and lifted my gun to Bates's forehead.

He made a pitiful sound in the back of his throat, his fat, squashed-in face shaking in terror.

"You tried to kill Jos last night, didn't you?" I snarled, getting up in his face. I flipped the safety off and put my finger on the trigger. "You ran her off the road. Didn't you?"

"N-No," he said, shaking his head adamantly. "It wasn't me, man. I swear to you."

"Then who?"

"I-I don't know. But...but I read the report the deputy wrote up. It sounded a lot like Fontana's truck." He was trembling now, and the memory of him standing over me back at Fontana's place in Eureka flooded through my head.

Raven's hand wrapped around my arm. "Tanner, please, don't kill him yet. If Lexa isn't there, we need him to help us find her." Her voice was imploring, trembling ever so slightly, telling me just how close to the edge she really was. "Please, you can do whatever you want with him when I have my baby back."

I hesitated, wanting just to be done with it and have this bastard out of my life for good. But then I looked into her eyes, saw her desperation, and slowly lowered my hand. I started to turn away, but I changed my mind at the last second and punched him dead center in the stomach.

He bowed over, vomiting all over his feet.

"We ready?" Bash asked everyone as they finished discussing the plan.

"Yeah," I agreed.

Bates was standing upright once again, and there was no way he'd missed any of the details. Trigger ran on ahead to find the best spot. We waited for the signal and pushed Bates up in front of us. He would get in, and Trigger would have his eye on him from a distance, his sniper rifle trained on Bates the whole time.

The rest of us followed at a slower pace, including Raven. Bash wanted her to stay behind, but there was no reasoning with her. Lexa was in there, and she was going to get her baby back one way or another.

The house was an old ranch-style design. The roof looked like it needed to be replaced—a decade ago. One really hard snow and it would cave in from the looks of it.

Colt, Raider, and Hawk moved around to the back door, getting into place first, while the rest of us took the front. Raven was stuck between Bash and Jet, but she had her own gun, and I almost pitied Fontana when she got to him.

Almost.

"Now!" Bash whisper-shouted and kicked in the front door just as an echoing sound came from the back of the house.

I knew where I was going simply from following the sound of Fontana screaming at Bates. Bash and Jet barreled through the house in front of me, but Raven slipped past them, making them both shout in protest.

The three of us reached her just as she lifted her gun and pulled the trigger.

Fontana jerked, then fell to his knees as his head canted around to glare at her. Blood poured out of his mouth seconds later, and she pulled the trigger again, this time hitting him in the face.

That was when I saw Lexa, and there was no mistaking the fact that Raven had already seen her. Because as soon as Fontana's brains were exploding out of the back of his head, Raven dropped her gun and was across the room and falling to her knees, her hands trembling as she ran them over the bruised, unmoving form of her daughter.

But it was the cut on her face, leaving her beautiful skin covered in blood, that had us all turning to stone. Fuck. He'd cut her. I didn't know how bad it was from where I was standing, but Raven was going crazy.

"Lexa," she shouted, feeling for a pulse. "Baby, open your eyes for Mommy. Look at me, Lexa. Please, look at me!"

Bash lifted the little girl into his arms, bracing her against his chest and took off running, his wife right behind him.

Bates just stood there in the middle of the living room, Fontana's blood and brains on his face and clothes. I crossed the distance separating us in seconds, lifted my gun, and put a single bullet in his brain.

Stepping back, I spat on both bodies at my feet and walked away.

It was over.

And I could finally breathe.

CHAPTER TWENTY FIVE

I couldn't stop shaking.

Not when I held Lexa in my arms in the back of Quinn's car and Bash drove like the hounds of hell were chasing us to the nearest hospital. There was so much blood. So many bruises.

Not when the doctor and a team of nurses took her from us when we ran into the ER, shouting for help. I screamed at them to let me go with her, my heart beating so hard it was close to exploding because I couldn't fucking stand to be away from her.

Not during the long wait, or when the cops arrived because we'd walked in with an unconscious, badly beaten child. We answered their questions. Told them who to call if they really needed to know so badly—Vito Vitucci, his son, his son-in-law. They always came up with a cover story to protect their muscle. They would sort the cops all out. Get these damn pigs out of my face so I could just worry about my daughter.

Not when the doctor finally came out to tell us what was going on and that Lexa was being rushed up to surgery.

Contusions. Broken bones. Internal bleeding. Severe concussion.

She'd been beaten to within an inch of her life. If we hadn't gotten her to the hospital in time, she could have bled out from a lacerated liver and a ruptured spleen.

Bash held me close, telling me it was going to be okay. But I didn't believe him. Lexa had been so still, so fucking broken. And that cut. What the hell had he used to make that damn cut? What had he done to my sweet little angel?

I was still shaking when the surgeon came out and said Lexa was going to be okay.

And that was when the world went black.

***

When I opened my eyes again, it was to find Bash leaning over me, his eyes wet with tears as he cradled my head in his huge hands. "Baby," he sobbed. "Thank fuck."

"Lexa!" I cried, sitting up so fast, the world began to spin.

Bash eased me back, carefully holding me. "She's in recovery. The doctor said we can see her as soon as she starts coming out from under the anesthesia," he reminded me. "You scared the hell out of me."

The shaking was starting to take hold of me again, but it was worse now. My teeth began to chatter together, my entire body feeling as if it was encased in ice. "Why can't I stop shaking?" I demanded, irritated.

"Reaction. Shock. You're coming down off some pretty high adrenaline, baby." He moved back then stood before lifting me to my feet.

He pulled off his coat and wrapped it around my shoulders, carefully pulling my hair out from under it and then folding his arms around me.

That was when I broke. When the lump filled my throat and the tears burned my eyes. I buried my face in his chest, and he gave me his strength as I let the stress and pain and agony of the last six-plus hours go.

It wasn't until Jet and the others arrived at the hospital that I was finally able to get some semblance of control over myself and wipe away my tears. By then, Bash's shirt was soaked in my tears and snot, but he didn't seem to care as we moved into the corner of the OR waiting room and the guys filled us in on what had happened after we'd left.

They had cleaned up the mess I'd created when I blew the man's face off.

I wasn't sorry. I knew I was supposed to feel some kind of remorse for taking a life, but all I felt was this overpowering sense of relief. Fontana couldn't hurt us anymore. Bates wouldn't get in our way again.

That wouldn't have mattered, though, if Lexa hadn't made it out of there alive. I would have wanted to follow them to hell and spend eternity tormenting the fuck out of them.

A nurse appeared in the doorway, glancing around. There were two other families waiting on their loved ones to get out of surgery, but somehow, I knew she was looking for us.

I moved forward and she frowned, probably wondering if I could possibly be the mother of the little girl who was under her care. Lexa and I looked nothing alike, but even though we didn't share a single drop of blood, she was mine just as much as Max was. Legally, I was her mother, but it was more than that. In my soul, she belonged to me.

Then she saw Bash behind me and understanding cleared her eyes. Lexa and Max both looked so much like their father, there was no denying who they belonged to.

"Mr. and Mrs. Reid?" I nodded. "Your daughter is starting to come around, and she keeps crying for her mommy. Would you like to follow me, and I'll take you back to her?"

I was already on her heels before she could clear the door.

Lexa was in the ICU, where the doctor told us she would be for the next day or so just as a precaution. She wasn't the most critical patient in the ward, but she was definitely the youngest.

When I saw her again, my heart stopped at just how badly Fontana had beaten her. There wasn't a single inch of skin that wasn't covered in bruises. Her face was stitched, the jagged cut going from her temple down to the corner of her mouth, disfiguring the entire right side of her face.

Rage filled me anew, and I wanted to kill the monster who did this to my baby all over again.

She was whimpering as the doors opened, and I rushed forward. Her blue eyes opened, and she started to cry as soon as she saw me. "Mommy!" But when she tried to sit up to hug me, she cried out in pain, and I bent so I could hug her, hold her.

I kissed her forehead carefully, brushing her hair back from her face, and just soaked up the fact that my daughter was alive.

CHAPTER TWENTY SIX

GRACIE

I closed down my computer and was about to get to my feet when my office door was pushed inward and Jenkins came in, a bottle of champagne in his hands.

With everything that had happened over the weekend, then rushing to clean up all the legal loose ends that went along with it, I was exhausted. Monday had passed in a blur at the neighboring county's police station and then the courthouse to make sure Hawk and the others hadn't faced any backlash after rescuing little Lexa.

Today, Tuesday, had been just another day to my exhausted brain and the constant morning sickness that was my new companion. But upon seeing my boss and mentor's grin and the gleam in his eyes, the realization of what this day really was hit me.

"Are the election results in?" I asked. As busy as things were, I was glad I'd voted absentee since there was no way I could have made it to the polls today.

"How about treating your new mayor to a steak dinner?" he asked, popping the top on his champagne.

I jumped up, throwing my arms around his neck. "I knew you would win!" I cried, hugging him tight.

"I don't know why I doubted myself so much," he grumbled, but he was still grinning. Setting the bottle down on the edge of my desk, he hugged me back before pulling away to grab my coat off the rack by my door. "Now, come on, woman. We have to talk business, and I'm starving."

I let him help me put on my coat then grabbed my briefcase as we left the office. His girlfriend had already left for the day, which surprised me. They should have been celebrating together, having a raging party as the town breathed a sigh of relief that Royce Campbell wasn't going to step into Derrick Michaels's shoes and take over where the other bastard had left off.

But I also knew that with Jenkins now the mayor, I would be taking over the law practice fully. It had always been part of the plan. When I started working for him years ago, it was written into my contract. I would work for him, learn from him, and then when he finally retired, he would have someone to inherit the practice.

Of course, I hadn't realized at the time that it was all a scheme thought up by Hawk and the MC to give me enough money to pay for law school. Now that I looked back on it, I was thankful they'd done what they had. I probably wouldn't have accepted the offer at the time if I had known, and I would have missed an incredible opportunity and the chance to learn from the best.

Jenkins opened the passenger door to his Audi and waited for me to get in before walking around to the driver's side. On the ride to Aggie's, we discussed all his open cases and what I would need to do to get caught up on them so I could step in. He knew I wouldn't have any issues, but he was still like an overprotective father. Not of his clients, but of me.

We pulled up outside Aggie's, and we were still talking about work as we walked in, so when everyone in the place screamed "Congratulations!" I nearly jumped out of my skin.

The entire town was laughing, throwing out praise and congrats. And for the next hour, instead of talking work, we celebrated.

"What's the first change you're going to make?" I asked when it was finally quiet enough to hold a conversation.

"First, I think I need to appoint a new sheriff until the spring election," he said with a laugh. "Bates taking off for the wild blue yonder after you found out he was being paid by some unsavory people means we're going to need a new official."

I snickered. "The pussy."

In my gut, I knew Bates was no more, but I had to pretend to believe like everyone else—that he'd just pulled up and left rather than face an internal investigation. If I didn't, I wouldn't be able to defend any of the MC guys if his body was ever found. But that was a huge *if*.

Hawk and his men weren't stupid. They wouldn't leave any evidence of Bates behind.

I should have been upset even to be thinking about having to defend the father of my unborn child for the previous sheriff's death, but it didn't even faze me. I wasn't sure what that said about me, but I'd learned not to give a damn since meeting Hawk Hannigan.

By the time I got home, I was dog-tired but all too happy to be back at the house. Hawk was still at the bar, the construction to patch up all the damage caused to it by the shootout a while back already underway. With Jet still at the hospital with Bash and Raven to watch over Lexa, Hawk and the other two Hannigan brothers had been overseeing the work that had been scheduled to start the day before.

With Fontana now no longer a problem, lockdown was officially over, and everyone had returned to their homes. Quinn and Kelli were in the kitchen when I walked in.

"Heard Jenks won," Quinn said with a grin as I dropped my purse and briefcase on the kitchen table. "Best news of the year."

"Agreed," I said with a laugh as I pulled a bottle of water out of the fridge. "It doesn't even matter that I'm about to start working sixty-hour weeks until I catch up on all his cases."

"You better take it easy, though," Kelli warned. "All that work stress isn't good for the baby."

I rubbed my hand over my still nonexistent baby bump. "Don't worry about that. Work is nothing compared to the last few weeks."

"Well, as long as you have enough time to hit pause and come to my wedding in two weeks, I'll be happy," Quinn said as she finished putting away the last of the dishes. "I can't get married without all my new sisters."

"I wouldn't miss it for anything," I assured her and grabbed my things. "I need a shower. See you two in the morning."

Twenty minutes later, I was collapsing into bed, so exhausted, I was already falling asleep when my head hit the pillow...

"Shit," Hawk growled low, probably trying to keep from waking me up.

I turned over in bed, already reaching for him, only to find the bed still empty. "Where are you?" I mumbled sleepily.

"Tripping over your damn briefcase," he grumbled seconds before his heavy body dropped down onto the mattress beside me. "We talked about you leaving it lying around, woman. What if you were the one to trip on it?" His hand swatted my rear. "You want to risk falling and hurting yourself or the baby?"

I snuggled deeper into the pillow, hiding my grin. "Sorry," I said...for the hundredth time. Knowing it would happen a hundred more times before I ever learned my lesson. I tended to drop my briefcase wherever and ignored it until I needed it or had to go to work.

"Why do I feel like your 'sorry' isn't sincere?" he huffed as he stretched out beside me and pulled me against his hard body. For weeks, we'd done this back at the clubhouse, but it hadn't felt as right as it did in that moment. Maybe it was because we were home again, or maybe it was just because the stress of Fontana and his crap was finally over. Whatever the reason, it made me happy.

But with the shot of happiness came the sudden flash of grief.

Jack.

I missed him so much.

A small sob left me before I even realized I was crying, and Hawk was suddenly turning on the lights so he could see my face. "Gracie, what's wrong?" he demanded, his voice gruff. "Baby, why are you crying?"

I buried my face in his chest, clinging to him. "I miss him," I whispered. "It doesn't feel right to be so happy when he's gone."

"Ah, baby, I know. I miss him too." He kissed the top of my head, his fingers stroking down my back soothingly. "Uncle Jack was like a second dad to me. I thought he was going to be around forever."

"I didn't get to tell him about the baby." I hiccupped, my tears falling faster. "He was going to be a great-grandfather, and he didn't even know."

"I wish I could have saved him for you, Gracie." He kissed the top of my head, his arms tightening around me protectively.

I lifted my head, letting the tears continue to fall, but frowning down at him. There was something in his voice that bothered me. "It wasn't your fault, Hawk. There was nothing anyone could have done."

"Maybe if I'd noticed he was off earlier in the day—"

I pressed my mouth to his, stopping his pained words. I kissed him long and hard, wanting to erase those thoughts from his head. When I lifted my head again, I cupped his jaw in one hand. "There was nothing you could have done," I repeated. "Don't beat yourself up over this, okay?"

"I hate it when you're so sad," he muttered. "It kills me to see your tears."

"You can't keep things from hurting me, babe. Life is full of too much pain for you to even try. Just hold me like you're doing now, and I'll be just fine," I assured him.

He lifted his lips in a grim smile. "I'll die holding you, woman. It's the only way I want to go."

Shaking my head at him, I laid my head back on his chest, letting the sound of his heart beating in my ear lure me back to sleep.

"If it's a boy, can we call him Jack?" Hawk asked before I could fall under sleep's spell.

My eyes snapped open, but I didn't move. "I love you so much."

"That a yes?"

I let my lashes fall again. "That's a definite yes."

CHAPTER TWENTY SEVEN

 JOSIE

The scent of coffee permeated the air as I opened the bathroom door and walked barefoot back to my room. The bedroom I had at Grandpa's didn't have a bathroom, and I wasn't ready to move into his master bedroom yet. That would mean having to clean out all his things, and I just wasn't mentally prepared for that.

Reid's pack 'n play was against the wall in the corner of my small room, but my son wasn't asleep in there as he'd been all night. He must have climbed out while I was in the shower and crawled into my bed beside his father.

I stopped before I reached it, looking down at my two sleeping boys. Tanner's arm was wrapped around Reid, both of them on their sides, heads on the same pillow facing each other. Both of them had their mouths open in deep sleep, snoring slightly. Seeing them together like this made me feel all warm and fuzzy inside, and I swallowed the lump that threatened to choke me before making myself get dressed.

I had a morning full of work to accomplish before I went dress shopping with Quinn and the others that afternoon. Reid and Tanner were going to spend the day together, much as they'd done all week. They were bonding, growing closer and developing a tight father-son relationship that made me happier than I ever realized I could be.

In the kitchen, Dad was sitting at the table, a mug of black coffee in front of him as he ate a bowl of instant oatmeal and a slice of toast.

"Made some extra if you want it," Dad said as he focused on the food before him.

"Thanks." I poured myself a cup of coffee then grabbed a bowl of oatmeal. Thankfully, I'd been able to go grocery shopping the day before, so there was fresh fruit in the fridge. I grabbed a few freshly washed berries and tossed them on top, then squeezed a little honey over it.

Dropping down into a chair at the small kitchen table with my dad, I offered him a smile. "It's nice now that everything has finally calmed down, don't you think?"

He nodded but chewed his food for a lot longer than was necessary, and I knew he had something to say that he didn't want to voice. I pretended not to notice and ate my breakfast, waiting for him to speak.

I was nearly done with my coffee when he finally opened his mouth. "Your mom keeps asking when you're going to come home."

"Funny, she hasn't tried to call me once."

But I wasn't surprised she'd called Dad. It was one of her favorite pastimes, making him miserable. She was a total bitch, and not even I could stand her for more than an hour at a time. I didn't have a lot to do with her, and I never let her keep Reid after the one time she'd babysat and I'd come home to find him with blisters on his bottom after she'd left him in a wet diaper all day.

"She said she's called you, but you don't ever answer."

I stood, carrying my dirty dishes to the sink. "Daddy, Mom hasn't called me in weeks, maybe even months. I don't know what she's told you, but we aren't close. Please don't give me the guilt trip about respecting her and being a good daughter—"

"Joslyn." Dad's gruff voice caught me off guard, and I turned to face him, concerned.

He was still sitting at the table, his head in his hands, tears running down his face.

I rushed back to him, throwing my arms around his neck and hugging him tight. "Dad, what's wrong?"

"I thought you were going to leave again," he choked out. "The way she made it sound, you were just biding your time and wouldn't talk to her because you didn't know how to let me down easy about going back to Oakland."

I kissed his cheek, giving him a smile to help ease his fears. "Daddy, really? Why would I leave you again? Everything I've ever wanted is right here. I never wanted to be anywhere else."

"Swear?" he forced out in a voice rough with emotion.

I kissed his cheek again. "I swear. I would have happily stayed with you while I was growing up if anyone had dared ask what I wanted."

His arm went around me, an affectionate hug from my father that I wasn't used to. But seeing him cry wasn't something I'd ever seen him do either. "You and Reid are all I have now, Jos. It was ripping me apart thinking you were going to leave."

"There is no way in hell she's going anywhere." Tanner's voice boomed behind me, making me jump in surprise.

I straightened, my heart racing as I watched him walk into the kitchen in nothing but a pair of sweat pants. His hair was sticking up at all angles, but I liked it that way. I reminded me of how my hands had tangled in those dark locks while his head was between my legs all night long. Thank God Reid was such a sound sleeper, because I'd been unable to hold back my moans for the most part.

Glaring, Tanner stomped across the distance that separated us. "I'm telling you right now, Jos, you even try to leave, and I'm gonna spank your ass. You hear me, woman? No way in hell I'm letting you go. And that goes double for trying to take my son with you."

Lips twitching, I stood there fighting not to grin as he tried to keep up the angry look. But he couldn't hide the panic just below the surface, the fear that he might not be able to stop me.

I touched my hand to his chest, pressing my palm flat over his pounding heart. "If you could calm down for two seconds, you would have heard that I was telling Daddy I'm not going anywhere. What part of 'I'm where I want to be' don't you understand, Tanner?"

His shoulders almost drooped for a moment in relief, but when he spoke, it wasn't to me. "Butch, I want to marry your daughter."

"What?" I whisper-shouted.

But the two men ignored me. "You better treat her right. No cheating. No breaking her heart. Provide for her and my grandson, or I'll cut your throat. Feel me?"

Tanner nodded solemnly. "I'll always take care of them, and I'd walk out in front of a bus before I hurt either of them."

"Then, yeah, boy. You can marry her."

I stood there, stunned by the way they were talking like I wasn't even there. Like they weren't discussing Tanner wanting to marry me, promising things that were making my heart melt to the point I was dangerously close to passing out from it.

"But you better do it right. No running off and eloping. I want to walk my baby girl down the aisle."

"Fuck yeah, we're doing it right. Big cake, big dress. Big everything. My woman deserves all of that."

I gulped, trying to find my voice. "A-Am I invited into this conversation, or are you two just going to continue making plans for *my* wedding?" Putting my hands on my hips, I glared from one to the other. "And excuse you, but I haven't even been asked yet, let alone accepted."

Tanner shrugged and went over to the coffeepot. "Quinn and Raider are getting married next weekend. Don't want to show them up. Let's have the wedding in a month. You think that's enough time, Butch?'"

"I'll drop by Aggie's, get her to help with planning it. That should give her time to make the cake." Dad finished the last of his coffee and carried his cup to the sink. Grabbing his packed lunch, he headed for the door. "See you at work, Jos. Don't be late."

The door shut behind him, and I had to breathe deep to keep from screaming, only stopping myself because I didn't want to wake my sleeping child.

I marched up to Tanner who was leaning against the counter beside the coffeepot and poked him in the chest with my index finger. "Now, you listen here, Tanner Reid. I am not, under any circumstances, marrying you until you ask. I may love you, and I may be the mother of your son, but I will not—abso-fucking-lutely will not—marry you until you get on one knee and propose."

Something flashed in his eyes, but I turned away, grabbed my travel mug of coffee and stormed toward the door.

"Jos," Tanner called softly from behind me.

Hand on the knob, I turned, ready to blast him again, only to find him on one knee right behind me. My heart lifted into my throat, and tears burned my eyes as they spilled one by one over my lashes.

He grasped my hands in both of his. "I love you, Jos. You are the best thing to ever happen to me. I don't like the me I am without you. Please, baby. I know I'm not the best man in the world, but for you, I'll try. I'll do my damned best to make you happy and kill anyone who dares make you sad. I want to be your man now and always. Will you marry me?"

"I..." I sucked in a deep breath, trying to calm down. "I... Holy shit. I didn't think you would actually ask."

"If it's what you want, I'll always try my damnedest to give it to you." He lifted my hands, kissing each palm. "I love you so fucking much, Jos. Marry me."

I was so choked up, I couldn't speak. I just stood there, staring down at him with tears pouring out of me like a freaking fire hydrant, unable to answer.

Tanner's throat bobbed as he swallowed, and he tried to laugh off his unease. "Babe, I kind of need you to say yes, because I'm about to go insane here."

I threw myself against him, sending us both crashing to the floor. "Yes!" I cried, kissing his lips quick and hard. "Yes. Of course, I'll marry you. I love you."

His chest swelled with a deep inhale, a weak laugh leaving him when he blew it out. "Thank fuck. I was really scared there for a second."

"Idiot," I muttered, kissing him again and again. "The answer was always going to be yes."

CHAPTER TWENTY EIGHT

 QUINN

I should have been upset that it was raining—what bride wanted it to rain on her wedding day?

But I was so deliriously happy even to be marrying Raider Hannigan that a little rain didn't bother me.

The forecast had been calling for it all week, so it wasn't like I was surprised. Which was why we were having it inside. Flick and a few of the others had spent the last two days decorating the clubhouse and even set up an arbor in the main room, while Jet and some of the brothers helped put chairs in position for the ceremony. It looked like an entirely different place by the time they were done.

Kelli, Gracie, and Rory sat on my bed in the room where I'd spent far too much time over the past month or so. We were using the bedrooms to get ready, me in Raider's room and Raider in Colt's, getting dressed and waiting until it was time for the wedding to start.

Behind me, Flick and Jos were finishing up with my hair. They'd spent the last hour curling, braiding, and then pinning little crystals into place. Between my hair, makeup, and the princess-style dress I'd been able to find the week before, I felt like a queen.

"You look beautiful," Kelli said, her eyes skimming over me from head to toe and back again. "Seriously, babe. I have never seen anyone as gorgeous as you are right now."

Pleasure made my cheeks bloom pink. There wasn't a full-length mirror anywhere in the clubhouse, so I was going to have to take her word for it. Knowing she wouldn't lie to me about something as important as how I looked on my wedding day, I let Flick finish placing the last pin where it needed to go.

A tap on the door preceded Raven walking in with Lexa beside her. My heart broke seeing the lingering bruises on the little girl's exposed skin, but it was the angry red mess of her right cheek that had tears burning my eyes.

I'd asked her to be my flower girl, and she was dressed in the adorable little sparkly white dress Raven and I had picked out for her. But the tears on Lexa's face told me I was probably going to be without a flower girl today, and that was just fine. I wasn't going to make her do anything she wasn't comfortable with.

"Quinn," Raven started, her tone full of apology. "Lexa is having a hard day."

I moved away from the others and crouched down in front of mother and daughter. Lexa's head hung low, the tears just pouring down her sweet little face. "Hi there, princess," I murmured softly. "Not feeling well today?" She shook her head, a little hiccup leaving her as she sniffled. "It's okay, baby girl. You don't have to be my flower girl if you don't feel up to it. You look so pretty, though.

I wish I looked half as pretty in my dress as you do in yours."

"But you're so beautiful," she whispered, her voice breaking.

"Not nearly as beautiful as you, Lexa." I held out my arms, and she walked into them after only a small hesitation.

I hugged her close, being careful not to squeeze her too hard. Her body was still healing after her surgery, and the cast on her wrist was covered in signatures and stick figures where everyone had signed it. It seemed like the pain in her arm from the gunshot wound didn't even matter anymore after everything else she'd been put through, but an MRI while Lexa was still recovering in the hospital had shown that the muscles and tendons were fine, she was just going through some painful growth spurts.

Lexa only allowed me to hug her briefly before she was turning back to her mom and hugging her leg. "Can we go sit with Daddy now?" she whispered.

Raven's smile was full of love. "Whatever you want, baby." Taking her daughter's hand, she looked me over. "You really do look beautiful, Quinn."

As she opened the door to exit, Colt came into the room. Dressed in a suit with his cut thrown over it, he looked as handsome as ever. As soon as his eyes landed on me, he stopped, gulping hard. "Holy Christ, Quinnie. You look stunning."

I did a little twirl. "Do you think so?"

"I would never lie about that, sweetheart." He opened his arms to hug me, then thought better of it. "I better not wrinkle you. Kelli is glaring at me like she's going to slit my throat."

Kelli stood, pushing between my best friend and me. "She's been getting ready for over an hour. If you fuck up this perfection before she says 'I do,' you better believe I'll do some slicing and dicing."

He grinned, kissing her lips. "I guess I'll just have to muss you up instead."

She snorted, shoving him back. "Just walk the girl down the aisle, dummy. You can muss all you want later."

That was enough to have my heart racing. My palms began to sweat, and I suddenly didn't know what to do with myself. "Oh my God," I whispered as he offered me his arm. "I'm getting married."

He tilted his head to the side curiously. "I'm a little concerned you're just now realizing that, Quinnie."

"Shut up," I cried, slapping at his arm. "It just feels real all of a sudden."

"Well, let's make it official now that it's real." He grasped my hand gently and pulled it through his arm. "Time to get you hitched."

Every woman in the room rushed me, pressing their lips to my cheek lightly so as not to smear lipstick on me, then hurried out of the room to take their seats, leaving me with just Colt and Kelli when it was over.

Kelli made one last glance-over to make sure my gown was still in order and unwrinkled before opening the door once again. I was so nervous, I was trembling by the time we got to the cue point where one of the brothers was supposed to start the music.

But as my maid of honor headed down the makeshift aisle and we moved into position to start down the same path, a sense of calm washed over me. I closed my eyes, wondering if it was my mom's spirit telling me everything was going to be okay. That thought brought me peace.

Opening my eyes, I couldn't stop my gaze from going straight to Raider, who was standing at the arbor with Jet as his best man. Those green orbs caressed me from head to toe, and the look in his eyes made me feel like the only woman in the world. As I watched him watching me, I saw his throat work, his Adam's apple bobbing as he waited for me to come to him.

Our gazes locked as Colt and I started up the aisle, but I honestly couldn't remember taking a single step until I was right in front of Raider, less than a foot away from the man I'd loved since before I even knew what that word really meant. The entire moment felt surreal until Raider stepped forward and took my hand from Colt's.

He tugged me close, bending his head to brush his lips softly over mine. The small caress was so sweet yet incredibly intimate. Happy tears stung my eyes, my heart nearly bursting from how perfect this moment was.

When he lifted his head, Raider's eyes were glassy with his own tears, but he didn't try to hide them. "I love you, Quinn," he said loud enough for everyone to hear.

My chin trembled, but I smiled up at him. "I love you too."

A throat clearing had us both turning our heads to find the minister standing there with his cheeks pink. "Do you two still need me? You seem to be doing a pretty good job on your own."

Raider's shoulders shook as he laughed. "Sorry, Reverend. I got impatient." His hand dropped to my waist, turning us to face the man. "Please, begin."

***

The only downside to having a princess-style wedding dress was going to the bathroom. It was at least a two-person job, so I held off until I couldn't hold it any longer.

Flick and Raven were both free, thankfully, and they helped me to the bathroom. It felt so good to pee that I actually moaned as they held the skirt of my dress up on either side, causing the two other women to laugh.

"It's the little things," Raven said with a grin as she passed me some toilet paper. "When I was pregnant with Max, it was just short of orgasmic to empty my bladder."

When I was done, they fixed my skirt for me while I washed my hands. "I'm so tired," I confessed as we walked into the bedroom and headed for the door. "I feel like today has lasted a week, but in a good way."

"It was a beautiful wedding," Flick commented.

"As soon as you and Raider cut the cake, you can make a break for it," Raven assured me. "Your car is already packed, so you don't have to worry about getting your things. Then you can go to the hotel and crash before you have to fly out in the morning for your honeymoon."

She opened the door and started to walk out ahead of Flick and me when she stopped dead in her tracks, causing me to bump into her back. "Hey," I grumbled, trying to see what the problem was. "What's going on?"

Raven muttered something savage under her breath that I didn't catch and moved so fast, I nearly stumbled forward. Seconds later, I heard a shriek and looked down the hall to find my sister Whitney on the floor at Raven's feet. Raven's heel was on her stomach, pressing into her.

"Don't run away from me, you little cunt," Raven seethed. "I saw you trying to go into Colt's room. Is Raider in there? Huh? You think you're going to try to cause trouble? I'll be damned if I let you fuck up this day for Quinn and my brother." Raven's leg moved, her foot going from Whitney's stomach to her throat. "You've been slithering around this clubhouse trying to cause shit for too damn long. I'm tired of it. Get your shit and get the fuck out. Don't you ever let me see your face here or at a club function again, because if I do—"

Colt's door opened, surprising me further, and Raider walked out, confirming Raven's suspicions. I didn't even have time to think before

Raider was pulling his sister off the woman whose windpipe she was trying to crush under her heel.

Raven struggled, her legs kicking out as he lifted her and placed her on her feet away from Whitney.

I stood there, dumbfounded by the whole episode, my emotions in a whirlwind. I was angry and hurt that my sister would still try to chase after Raider even now that we were married. Those two emotions were the most intense of the ones trying to fight for dominance in my head at that moment.

Flick's soft hands touching my bare back jerked me out of my momentary stupor, and I stomped down the hall to where Raven was still trying to get past her brother. Whitney remained on the floor, coughing and silently crying.

"What the hell is wrong with you?" Raider demanded. "Whitney just told me she was sorry for all the shit she'd been doing lately. I told her to fuck off. I don't care if you beat the hell out of her, but could you please not kill anyone on my wedding day? I don't want to ruin this for Quinn."

"Then why did she run from me when she saw me?" Raven snarled.

"Probably because you look a little psychotic right now, Rave." He shook her shoulder firmly, trying to get her to control herself. "You have to calm down, Raven."

"But she… She…"

I wrapped my arms around Raven from behind, putting my head on her shoulder. "It's okay, Raven," I told her, my voice soft and soothing. "I believe Raider when he says she was just apologizing. Although she should have been apologizing to me, not to him." I shot my sister a glare, not feeling even an ounce of sympathy for her. "Get up, Whitney."

"I-I really am s-sorry," she stammered, scrambling to her feet. "Please, Raven. Don't banish me."

"Just go, Whitney," Raider snapped. "You mess with Quinn even once more, and I'll break your neck myself. I know that's what you were really hoping for, so be thankful I don't want to go to jail before I have my honeymoon."

She turned and ran, and even though my arms were still around my new sister-in-law, Raven tried to go after her.

"Raven, you have to chill out," Flick urged her in a quiet voice, pushing between Raider and Raven from the front.

All the rage seemed to deflate from her, and she went limp in my arms. "I can't help it," she whispered. "I'm just so damn angry all the time, Flick. All this rage, all this pain, I can't contain it, and I have to for Lexa's sake."

The other woman wrapped her arms around Raven from the front, the two of us trying to infuse all of our love for her into our hug. "I know, honey. I know," Flick told her, stroking a hand over her hair. "It's going to be okay, though. Lexa is going to be just fine, with you to help her through this."

"I just want to fix this for her, and I can't," she sobbed, burying her face in Flick's chest.

"She doesn't need you to fix it," Raider told his sister, standing there protectively. "She just needs you to love her. The rest will fix itself eventually."

She lifted her head, tears and snot running down her face. "When did you get so smart?" she tried to tease.

His green gaze caught mine. "It took a hell of a lot longer than it should have, but I eventually grew a brain." He turned his focus back on his sister. "Flick is right. Lexa will be just fine because you have her back, Raven. You're the most amazing mother I've ever seen. Maybe if she didn't have such a strong, loving mom to help her through this, I would be concerned, but she has you. So I'm not worried about her."

"I don't feel strong. I feel like I'm failing her."

"Well, you're not," a new voice growled, and I looked up to find Bash walking down the hall.

Seeing him, Raven quickly started wiping her face, trying to get rid of the evidence of her tears. But there was no hiding them from her husband. He saw them, and his blue eyes darkened. As he drew closer, I released her, and he gathered her in his arms. "You are the reason Lexa is even able to leave the house without having a panic attack. You are why she hasn't been crying herself to sleep since she left the hospital. You, Raven. You are her happy place, just as you are mine." He lifted her off her feet until their gazes were even. "Please don't cry, baby. Don't doubt yourself."

Flick and I shared a look, and we both nodded. I grasped Raider's hand, tugging him with us as we moved discreetly down the hall, letting the two have a moment of privacy.

"I-I think I just needed to beat the shit out of someone," Raven said with a shaky laugh.

"That's okay. Whitney deserved it. But next time you feel like you're about to explode like that, how about coming and finding me and we can just have really rough sex?" I heard the teasing in his voice, but I knew he was being completely serious.

Raider growled something under his breath, and Flick and I both laughed at him as we walked out of earshot of the couple. It wouldn't surprise me if we didn't see them again for a while.

"Can we go yet?" Raider complained as we reached the main room where everyone was eating, dancing, or just sitting around talking and having a good time.

A quick glance around the room told me Whitney had left, which was a good thing, because I was fairly sure Raven would have gone after her again if she saw her. My heart warmed at the realization I now had a sister who would have my back.

"You still have to cut the cake," Flick reminded him. "Do that, and then you can sneak out through the kitchen."

His arms lifting me off my feet had me squealing, catching the attention of everyone in the room. "Hey," he called out. "I'm cutting this damn cake, and then I'm taking my wife far, far away from you fuckers. So get your cameras out and take your damn pictures because I'm not waiting around a second longer than I have to."

My happy laugh filled the room as he carried me over to the table where the cake was, and he reluctantly placed me on my feet. Keeping one arm wrapped around my back, he picked up the knife. "Let's do this, beautiful."

With my hand over his, we cut the cake and then fed each other a small bite of it. I heard cameras snapping, flashes going off in all directions, but they weren't enough of a distraction to keep me from seeing just how hungry my husband was for me.

I grabbed his hand and pulled him toward the door, needing to be alone with him just as much as he did.

Behind us, everyone was already throwing birdseed and confetti as we ran from the clubhouse to my car that was parked right in front. Raider opened my door, making sure I was safely inside before jogging around to the driver's side. Thankfully, the rain had stopped for the moment. Everyone was screaming and cheering around us, but all I could see was him.

Today had been perfect, but tonight—that was going to be epic.

CHAPTER TWENTY NINE

Twenty weeks pregnant

I fought back a yawn as the bar filled up with MC brothers and their families. Today was going to be a celebration for everyone, and not just as a way to finally unwind from all the crazy that had been pressing down on us.

Shifting in my chair, I went to reach for my glass of lemonade on the table in front of me, only to have James beat me to it. He was standing two feet away, talking to Bash and Hawk, and his eyes hadn't even been on me. Yet as soon as I so much as thought about moving, he was there, anticipating my every need.

It was annoying, but every time he did it, I fell a little deeper in love with him.

His lips touched my brow before he returned to his conversation with the other two like nothing had even happened.

Rolling my eyes, I took a sip of my lemonade and set the glass on top of my stomach. With all three babies thriving, my stomach was growing more and more every day, but I was still months away from being full term. The other women who were just as far along in their pregnancies were barely showing, yet I looked like I could pop any day.

I was sure there were three beasts in there and not three tiny babies. No one could convince me otherwise. But I loved them with every fiber of my being, and I was anxious to meet each one of them.

Lexa pulled out the chair beside me, moving it close so she could lean her head against my shoulder. I kissed the top of her head, wishing I could take away the new sadness that had invaded my precious little niece's heart. If I didn't know that the man responsible for this new Lexa was already dead, I would have sent James out to slaughter any and all who'd had a hand in it, even inadvertently.

Raven set a paper plate full of all Lexa's favorite foods in front of her. "Here, baby. Eat and then we will have cake after the big babies' gender reveal," she said with an encouraging smile. "It's your favorite. Strawberry shortcake."

"Not hungry," Lexa mumbled, hiding the side of her face that was still red and tender against my stomach. "I just wanna go home, Mommy. Everyone keeps looking at me."

I felt Raven's tension, but she didn't let Lexa see a single sign of it. "No one is looking at you. They're looking at Aunt Willa's ginormous stomach. Can you believe you have three cousins in there? How is that even possible?" Raven placed her hands on my stomach, and I didn't mind her manhandling my belly for the sake of distracting the little girl beside me. "Holy crap, feel here, Lexa. This one is trying to kick his way out already."

Curious, Lexa lifted her head. Her dark hair fell forward, shielding the scar from onlookers. Carefully, she placed her hand beside her mom's and waited. As if on cue, one of the babies kicked at her hand, making her gasp in awe.

"Does that hurt?" she whispered in amazement.

"Nope," I lied. Yes, it hurt. Sometimes I was fairly sure those three were bruising my insides. Not that I would tell her or James that. "They kick me like this all the time. The only time it bothers me is when they kick my bladder and I have to go pee."

Considering I was on modified bed rest, that was more annoying than anything else. And considering it was hard to so much as wipe, I had to have constant help. Raven spent a lot of time at my house when James was at work, though, and when she wasn't around, one of my other friends was. Flick was just as much of a godsend as Raven was, and I would have died of mortification if my husband had to do half the things those two women helped me with every single day.

I picked up a slice of pineapple from Lexa's plate. "Sweet baby Jesus, this is so good," I groaned. "Taste, Lexa. Your momma picked the best pineapple in the entire grocery store."

Reluctantly, she took a slice and nibbled. Before long, she was eating a second piece and then moving on to the sandwich. Raven and I shared a look as Lexa quietly ate her lunch, both of us hurting for the little girl we loved more than life itself.

"Where do we put these?" Jet asked as he carried a huge box, one of three.

The week before, we'd done a gender reveal for both Quinn and Gracie, both of whom had left the bar overflowing with blue balloons. In the coming weeks, we would be doing one for Rory and, not shockingly, Jos. The way Tanner couldn't keep his hands off his new wife, it didn't surprise me that he'd already knocked her up again.

Raven straightened, directing her brother and the two other men to place the boxes full of balloons in the middle of the bar where a space had already been cleared. My hands began to itch, needing to know what color balloons were in each of those huge boxes. I had my suspicions they were all boys, but I really wanted there to be at least one girl swimming around in there. Not for my sake, but James's. I knew he wanted a daughter so bad he could taste it.

But we hadn't let the doctor or tech tell us when they were doing the latest scan just a few days before. We wanted to be just as surprised as everyone else. The only person who knew was Raven so she could put the boxes together, and she hadn't dared even hint at the secret she was keeping.

Glancing down at me, she smiled. "You ready for this?"

I nodded in a rush, causing her to laugh. Offering me her hands, she helped me stand carefully.

James glared at both of us as he broke away from Bash and Hawk again. "No standing."

"I think she'll be okay for the five minutes it will take to do the reveal, Spider," she told him with a roll of her green eyes. "Let her have a little fun. You keep claiming this is the only time she's going to get to do this, so let her enjoy it."

"Five minutes and not a second longer," he growled.

I beamed up at him. "Thanks, baby."

Raven positioned us right where she wanted us, each of us standing in front of a box, with one box left in the middle. The goal was to open the outside two at the same time, then do the middle one together. I was practically dancing with excitement as I waited for her to give the signal to open my box.

"Five. Four. Three. Two…" She paused, making me do a little growling of my own at her. Laughing, she cried, "One!"

I opened my box so fast, it took a moment for me to realize what color balloons flew toward the ceiling.

Pink!

I looked over at James and saw his eyes were on his own balloons.

Pink…

Wait.

I had been sure that every single baby was a boy. All the pink balloons kind of disappointed me a little. I wanted a son, someone who looked just like his daddy, whom I could dress in little jeans and miniature biker boots and leather jackets. I even had an online shopping cart full of all those things I wanted to dress our boys in.

"Last one," Raven said, urging me toward the middle box.

James had the biggest grin on his face as he bent to kiss me. "Best day of my life," he murmured by my ear.

The disappointment melted away at those words, and I leaned into him, soaking up all the love that was radiating off him.

Each of us put a hand on the box as Raven counted down again, and I was sure the entire room held their breath as they waited for us to open the box.

A dozen blue balloons floated up past my face, and I screamed in delight, only just barely containing the urge to jump up and down in my excitement. The whole bar was cheering, congratulating us, pounding James on the back like he'd done his job as a man and then some. It all had me rolling my eyes, but he was eating it up.

"You do realize I'm the reason we're having more than one, right? Different genders means more than one egg," I told him. "I feel like I should be the one getting a pat on the back here."

"Actually," Raven spoke up. "The notes on the scan said they were sure the girls are identical, so it seems like you're both responsible for these multiples."

"So there," Bash said with a laugh, teasing me like always. "You're both to blame."

James snorted, then picked me up in his arms. "Five minutes are up. Sit and stay there, or I'm taking you home." He placed me back in my chair then bent and kissed me. "This really is one of the best days of my life," he said as he pulled back. "Thank you for our life, Willa."

Emotions choked me as I grabbed his cut and jerked him back down when he would have straightened. "I love you so much, James."

EPILOGUE

Twelve years later

I picked up the last of the dishes and placed them in the sink. Breakfast had turned the place into a madhouse with the kids all running around. There were times when I loved sharing a house with Raven and Bash and their two kids, but now that Jet and I had kids of our own, mornings were a disaster, especially when it was a school day.

Lexa, Max, and my son were already on their way out the door before I could blink.

"Bye, Mom!" Garret called, slinging his backpack over his shoulder and grabbing his packed lunch off the counter. "Love you."

"Garret Hannigan!" I raged, following after him.

He froze less than two feet from the back door. Sighing dramatically, he turned and slowly walked back to me. I bent, hiding my grin as he kissed my cheek.

Max snickered on his way past. "Bye, Aunt Flick. See you later."

"Bye, Max," I called without taking my eyes off my son, who looked so much like his father, it literally made my heart ache. "I love you, mister."

Since he was nine, I was fairly sure having anyone hear that his mother loved him was embarrassing. I didn't care, though. He'd hear it a million times in the coming years. I wasn't going to stop saying those three words because he didn't like it.

"I love you too, Mom," he grumbled. "Can I go now?"

I blew out a sigh. "Go. Have a good day. Don't get in any fights." I knew I was wasting my breath. At least once a week, I was at his school, trying to talk the principal out of expelling him because he'd gotten into yet another fight. My third-grader was a hothead, but I was hoping he'd calm down eventually.

"Mommy!" I shut the door to find my daughter storming into the room, her iPad in her hand.

I stayed by the door, watching her with concealed amusement as she stalked toward me with attitude. Nova looked more like her Aunt Raven than me, and her personality was one hundred percent my best friend's.

"What's wrong?"

She thrust her iPad into my hands. An iPad neither her father nor I had given her. It was a present from her best friend, the boy who would have been attached to her hip if he didn't live on the other side of the freaking country.

Nova met Ryan Vitucci when she was three and Ryan was eight. Jet and I took the kids to visit my aunt Mary, and we'd spent a few weeks in New York one summer. It had been a great vacation, but Nova had thrown a fit when we told her we had to return home. As a going-away present, Ryan had given her an iPad.

So they could video chat.

They'd stayed in touch ever since. She saw and talked to Ryan more than she did her own brother. It was amusing, and I loved that she already had a friend she couldn't seem to live without.

"Take my iPad and hide it!" she commanded, crossing her arms over her chest.

I lifted a brow at her tone, and she quickly added, "Please, Mommy."

"Why should I hide your iPad?" I questioned, noticing the thing was turned off. Holy crap. I didn't know it could do that. It was never turned off. If she wasn't talking to Ryan on it, she was playing one of the hundreds of learning activities Ryan had helped her download before we left New York. Those games were annoying to hear at times, but they'd also been a godsend. She was beyond ready for kindergarten next year, and she was probably even more advanced than some second-graders. "You'll just whine for it in like ten minutes."

"No, I won't. I'm mad at Ryan! I'm not talking to him ever again." Her little chin trembled, my only warning before she burst into tears.

Startled by her sudden change in emotions, I scooped her up. She was so tiny, it was hard to believe she was about to turn five in just a few more days. Having a birthday in November kept her from entering school for another year, but I was glad for the extra time. I needed it more than she did, because I wasn't sure I was ever going to be ready to let her leave my side.

Nova was my baby, and after how difficult my pregnancy had been with her, she was our last. I'd had a hysterectomy the moment the doctors pulled her from me via C-section, something that had saved my life. I hadn't had a choice because I was bleeding out so badly. Jet had been a mess, but we'd had other things to worry about at the time since Nova was eight weeks early.

Thankfully, though, her small size was the only issue she now had. But fuck, it had been scary for that first year.

Cuddling her close, I carried her into the living room and sat on the couch with her in my lap. "What's wrong, sweetie?" I asked, getting more than a little emotional myself because her tears always wrecked me.

"Ry-Ryan is so mean!" she cried, pressing her snotty nose into my shoulder and using my shirt as her tissue.

I blinked down at her, unsure she was talking about the same Ryan who was her best friend. Maybe she'd met a new Ryan, because the one I knew adored her too much to ever make her think he was mean. Perhaps he was—hell, I'd never seen him around any kids other than my own and his cousins, but what I had seen of his interactions with them showed me he was a nice enough boy.

"Okay, maybe you should tell me everything that happened, Nova."

"He's supposed to come to my birthday party, but when I talked to him just now, he said he couldn't." She scrubbed at her eyes, getting mad all over again.

"This is the first I'm hearing that they're canceling," I told her. "Maybe you heard him wrong."

Her birthday party had been all she could talk about for the past few months, ever since Ryan and his mother had flown out for a few days so Ryan and Nova could spend a little time together. They'd promised to come back for the party in November, and she'd been meticulously planning it ever since.

"Ryan said his mommy is sick. She just found out she's going to have a baby, and they can't come because she's got a tummy ache." Nova sighed like her heart was breaking. "If he won't come to my party, then I won't be his friend anymore."

"Nova," I scolded gently. "Ryan's mom has been trying really hard to have a baby. You should be happy that he's going to be a big brother."

"But my heart hurts, Mommy. I miss him so, so, so, so much. I just wanted him to come to my party."

Her broken little sobs hurt me, and I was thankful Jet was already at the bar doing inventory. If he heard his baby girl crying like she was right then, he would have lost his damn mind. If Nova wasn't happy, Jet Hannigan was not happy, and that could be dangerous for everyone in a two-hundred-mile radius.

I rubbed her back, hoping she would calm down so I wouldn't be tortured by those little sniffled hiccups for long. "Honey, Ryan can't help that his mom is sick. You need to be a little more understanding. I'm sure he doesn't want to disappoint you, but he is really close to his mom and he's going to want to stay close to her when she's not feeling well."

"I know, but I miss him," she sobbed.

Hugging her close, I kissed the top of her head, rocking her gently. "I'm so sorry, Nova."

It took an hour before she would stop crying, and even when her tears dried up, she was clingy. I had errands to run and things to do around the house before the kids came home from school. Bash was always at work by seven every morning, and since both Raven's kids were in school now, she had taken over the office at what had once been Uncle Jack's garage, which Trigger and Bash co-owned now.

I loved staying home with the kids, taking care of the house, and dealing with the day-to-day things like helping with homework. It was everything I'd ever wanted, but it was an extremely busy job, one that never ended.

Nova stayed quiet during our errand-running, not even singing along to the radio like she normally would have. Ice cream was turned down, as was her favorite lunch at Aggie's. I decided to make her favorite dinner that night, but she barely lifted her head when I suggested it.

As always, I picked the three kids up from school and drove us home. They all had homework, and Lexa and Max always did that on their own. Garret, however, had to be constantly watched, or he would use his homework pages as target practice and use his pencils for darts. It was a constant chore with that boy.

By the time dinner was ready, Bash and Raven were home. Jet was helping me set the food on the table when the doorbell rang. Since my hands were the only ones empty, I went to answer it.

It took me a few seconds to realize the little boy on the doorstep was real and not a figment of my imagination. I glanced behind him, expecting to see half a dozen men in suits with guns under their jackets. Or a little Russian woman, at the very least. Neither were here. There wasn't even a car in the driveway to give me a clue me how this kid got here.

"Hi, Mrs. Hannigan," Ryan greeted with a tired smile. His brown eyes were full of sadness and worry so thick it was hard to believe he was only ten. My cousin Ciro's wife Scarlett had told me just what this little boy had gone through when he was little more than a baby. His biological mother had been a monster, and I was glad she was dead. "Can I speak to Nova, please?"

"I... Umm..." I shook my head, trying to clear it as I realized he was actually there. "Ryan, what are you doing here? Where are your parents?"

He shrugged. "Mom wasn't feeling well because she's having bad morning sickness, and Papa is in Chicago on business."

"Then how did you get here?"

"We have two private planes. I used Mom's phone to have the pilot get the one Papa wasn't using ready by text and then called a private car company to take me to the airport. A second car service was waiting when I landed." He shrugged again, like it was nothing. Like he hadn't just traveled thousands of miles by himself.

I wouldn't trust Garret to walk to the end of the block by himself.

"Does your mom know you're here?" I demanded, my heart pounding, imagining either of my children just taking off like that.

"I didn't want to worry Mom."

"Oh my God," I whispered. Anya was going to lose her fucking mind.

I grabbed his shoulder, bringing him into the house even as I pulled my phone out of my back pocket. Fingers shaking, I hit my cousin's contact number. Seconds later, Ciro's deep voice filled my ear.

"I don't have time to chat, Felicity," he said, sounding out of sorts. "I have a problem here and—"

"Ryan?" I breathed.

"Yeah... How did you know?"

I shook my head at the little boy in front of me. "Just a guess. Oh, and by the way, I have a new houseguest. Ryan just showed up at my front door."

He blew out a relieved breath. "Thank God. Anya was going ballistic. We thought someone kidnapped him. Cristiano is in Chicago, and he was about to blow up the world."

I could only imagine. "What should I do with him?"

"Just keep him there. I'll let Cristiano know, and he can fly over to pick him up instead of coming home." He blew out another long breath. "Can I speak to him?"

Ryan took the phone when I offered it to him. As he listened, his face didn't change once, even though I could clearly hear Ciro yelling at him.

"I'm sorry Mom was upset. I didn't mean to make her worry. That's not what I wanted. I just didn't want Nova to be sad."

My heart actually melted at how sweet this kid was. He was so caring, so sincere, it brought tears to my eyes. I couldn't be upset with him now; that was impossible.

And if I were honest, I was glad he'd come. Nova had been a shell of her normal self all day, but I knew when she saw her best friend, she would be okay again.

Ryan patiently listened to his uncle snarling at him for a few more minutes before hanging up and offering me the phone back. "Can I see Nova now, Mrs. Hannigan?"

Ruffling his hair, I nodded. "Sure, buddy."

I led the way to the kitchen where everyone was already sitting but hadn't started eating yet.

Jet was watching for me, his brow puckered when his gaze caught mine. "Who was it?"

"Well…" I stepped aside, letting them see our new guest.

"Ryan!" Nova screamed. She was out of her seat and across the room in a matter of seconds.

She was a tiny little thing, but she threw herself against him so forcefully, Ryan fell back, being careful not to let her hit her head as she fell beside him, laughing.

"You said you couldn't come," she cried. "Did you lie to me? I don't care. I'm just happy you're here."

"I didn't lie," he assured her. "I didn't want you to be sad, so I came without telling anyone. I think I'm in trouble, but I don't care. It was worth it to get to see you smiling at me like that."

I heard Jet muttering something savage, and I hid my grin. Daddy was definitely seeing what I was seeing.

I just hoped he could survive it.

Playlist

"I Will Return" by Skylar Grey

"The Madness" by Art of Anarchy

"Into the Fire" by Asking Alexandria

"Dangerous Woman" by Ariana Grande

"I Am a Stone" by Demon Hunter

"Monster" by Eminem ft. Rihanna

"River" by Eminem ft. Ed Sheeran

"Call Me When You're Sober" by Evanescence

"Irresistible" by Fall Out Boys

"Remember Everything" by Five Finger Death Punch

"Rock Bottom" by Hailee Steinfeld

"Castle" by Halsey

"Moth" by Hellyeah

"Right Here in My Arms" by HIM

"Bad Things" by Machine Gun Kelly & Camila Cabello

"In the Name of Love" by Martin Garrix & Bebe Rexha

"Just a Dream" by Nelly

"Angel With a Shotgun" by Night Core

Next from Terri Anne

Needing Forever VOL 1
Needing Forever VOL 2
(Novella Collections featuring favorite secondary characters from The Rocker... Series)

Chasing Hope
(Standalone)

Angels Halo Next Gen Series
Salvation *(Lexa)*

Rockers' Legacy
Holding Mia
Needing Nevaeh

Printed in Great Britain
by Amazon

40781730R00210